THE INCREDIBLE DIARY OF...

South Yorkshire

Edited By Daisy Job

First published in Great Britain in 2019 by:

Young Writers
Remus House
Coltsfoot Drive
Peterborough
PE2 9BF
Telephone: 01733 890066
Website: www.youngwriters.co.uk

All Rights Reserved
Book Design by Ben Reeves
© Copyright Contributors 2019
SB ISBN 978-1-78988-634-4
Printed and bound in the UK by BookPrintingUK
Website: www.bookprintinguk.com
YB0408L

Foreword

Dear Reader,

You will never guess what I did today! Shall I tell you? Some primary school pupils wrote some diary entries and I got to read them, and they were EXCELLENT!

They wrote them in school and sent them to us here at Young Writers. We'd given their teachers some bright and funky worksheets to fill in, and some fun and fabulous (and free) resources to help spark ideas and get inspiration flowing.

And it clearly worked because WOW!! I can't believe the adventures I've been reading about. Real people, make-believe people, dogs and unicorns, even objects like pencils all feature and these diaries all have one thing in common – they are JAM-PACKED with imagination!

We live and breathe creativity here at Young Writers – it gives us life! We want to pass our love of the written word onto the next generation and what better way to do that than to celebrate their writing by publishing it in a book!

It sets their work free from homework books and notepads and puts it where it deserves to be – OUT IN THE WORLD! Each awesome author in this book should be **super proud** of themselves, and now they've got proof of their imagination, their ideas and their creativity in black and white, to look back on in years to come!

Now that I've read all these diaries, I've somehow got to pick some winners! Oh my gosh it's going to be difficult to choose, but I'm going to have SO MUCH FUN doing it!

Bye!

Daisy

Contents

Coit Primary School, Chapel Town

Isaiah McKenzie Lee (8)	1
Amelia McDonald	2
Oliver James Haine (7)	4
Oz Leonidas Edward Hiley (8)	6
Zackary Round (8)	8
Totie Fong (7)	10
Oscar Hudson (8)	12
Cole Michael Mullan (8)	14
Lewis Mellors (7)	16
Lucy Ball (8)	17
Spencer Mounsey (8)	18
Sriyan Sen (7)	19
Lucy Iris Sykes (8)	20
Olivia Rose Batty (8)	21
Scarlet Boothby (8)	22
Olly Gillott (8)	23
Oliver Colville (7)	24
Kayla Davis (7)	25
Owen Lever (8)	26
Harvey Poulter (8)	27

Greasbrough Primary School, Greasbrough

Amelia Cook (10)	28
George Lee Henderson (8)	30
Kara May Bentley (7)	32
Leah Joanne Hardwick (10)	34
Libby Exley (9)	36
Nell White (10)	38
Jack Portman (9)	40
Selina Royala Smith (8)	42
Madison Willers (9)	44

Ava Jessica Frier (8)	46
Kayla McErlean (8)	47
Megan Lily Wright (8)	48
Sophia Barlow (8)	50
Zeynep Beyza Sargin (8)	51
Heidi Florence Astle (10)	52
Dylan James Currie (7)	53
Jack Clay (7)	54
Imogen Ashcroft (8)	55
Jake Elliott (8)	56
Anna Sofia Kurti (9)	57
Megan Evison (8)	58
Arran Curran (8)	59
Lily May Williams (9)	60
Eva Natasha Sanderson (9)	61
Olivia Craven (8)	62
Reece Cobi Hazelhurst (10)	63
Anthony Peter Roddis (11)	64
Beatrice Bradley (10)	65
Yazmin Dewick (9)	66
Ella Rose Williams (9)	67
Tristan Allan (10)	68
Darcey Flint (7)	69

Hatchell Wood Primary Academy, Bessacarr

Zainab Ul-Hassan (10)	70
Millie Taylor (10)	72
Ryan (10)	74
Amelia Mccormack (10)	76
Devon Farthing (10)	78
Yuvraj (10)	80
Freya Rose Webster (10)	82
Alys Catherine Spencer (10)	84
Adam (10)	86

Jayden Samuel Ross (9)	88
Paige Lucas (10)	89
Reece (9)	90
Joshua Wilkin (10)	91
Lars (9)	92
Sarah (10)	93
Szofia Buhajcsuk (10)	94
Katie Lynne Hoyle (10)	95
Rio (10)	96
Ebony Angel Tucker (10)	97
Marie Walton (9)	98
Sarena Collin (10)	99
Jack (10)	100
Ashton Griffin	101
Avah Grace Evans (10)	102
Joshua (10)	103
Melissa Malam (10)	104
Cruz Walter Dodds (9)	105
Hayden Snodin (10)	106

Hatfield Academy, Sheffield

Saif Ally (9)	107
Oliver Sampson (8)	108
Ruby Jean Broomhead (9)	110
Al-Sadig Bakhit (9)	112
Sarah Ahmed Maisari (9)	114
Phoebe Crookes (9)	116
Leila Zeb (9)	118
Amelia Isobell Lucas (9)	120
Brooke Stringer (9)	122
Tyler Memmott (9)	124
George Lyall (9)	126
Sharifah Wright (9)	127
James Fu (8)	128
Emma Isabella Pyecroft (9)	129

Serlby Park Academy, Bircotes

Lucy Johnson (7)	130
Esther Clarke (8)	132
Mary-Beth Stephenson (11)	134

St Oswald's Academy, Finningley

Sophia Sana (9)	135
Darcie Mae Whitaker (8)	136
Gregor Scott (9)	138
Harris Chapman (8)	140
Joseph Baker (9)	142
Kathryn Rose Beasley (9)	144
Avilon Pawson (8)	146
Lilla Rose Ward (9)	147
Oliver Storey (9)	148
Geno Eagle (9)	149
Alfie Harrison Taylor (9)	150
Harry Hermiston (8)	151
Eleanor Spencer (9)	152
Joseph Duncan (9)	153
Alex Austin (9)	154
Maximillian Jorge Lunn (9)	155
Kyle James Williams (9)	156
Jake Raggett (8)	157

Totley All Saints CE Primary School, Sheffield

Megan Wright (10)	158
Darcy Booth (11)	160
Harrison Corrin (10)	162
Megan Hill (11)	164
Evie Staniforth (10)	166
Isabel Campsill (11)	168
Lily Grayson (11)	170
Guy Eckersley (10)	172
Evie Dastoor (10)	173
Rachel Holme (11)	174
Sizhe Luo (11)	175
Samuel Giles (11)	176

West Meadows Primary School, Hoyland

Coby Hopkinson (8)	177
Alisha Moxon (8)	178
Cady Morrison (7)	180
Oliver Jack Turner (8)	182

Charlotte Grace Jones (8)	184
Leon Himsworth (7)	186
Lily Morgan (7)	188
Georgia Holly Marsh (8)	190
Keira Grace Pepper (8)	192
Myla Fannan (7)	194
Calum Warren (8)	195
Fynley Blade Young (8)	196
Claudia McDonald (8)	197
Paige Manners (8)	198
Alfie Briggs (7)	199

Worsbrough Bank End Primary School, Worsbrough Dale

Daniel Saukaitis (11)	200
Lilyblue Monteith Walker (11)	202
David Saukaitis (11)	204
Connor Paul Williams (11)	206
Thomas Adam Elbourne (10)	208
Joel Bobby Besau (10)	209
Demi-May Williams (11)	210
Hamish Monteith Walker (11)	211

The Diaries

The Great Adventure

Dear Diary,
My name is Tom and I have found a portal on my great adventure today. So you bet I am lying, but I am not. So I was going on holiday with my family. I was going to have a swim and then a huge, grey, purple portal appeared in front of me. I stood there for a minute and said to myself, "Shall I go in and would my Mum like not seeing me in a while?" I thought yes, so I stepped into the portal and it took me to a lost land. I could see dancing leaves and the mini gummy frogs jumping in the chocolatey swamp. The sugary wind blew in my face while I was eating the chocolate grass. "Mmmm yummy."
The candyfloss clouds changed colour every minute, that helped me know what time it was and when I had to go back. Then I saw someone walking towards me, it was my little sister. She said, "Where are we, Tom?"
I replied, "I call it the great adventure."
Then me and my little sister stepped back into the portal and said to our Mum, "We have been on a great adventure today."

Isaiah McKenzie Lee (8)
Coit Primary School, Chapel Town

The Candy Land

Dear Diary,
Today has been the best day ever because my dream came true. I went to a world of candy which was my dream. The stars were shining like Starbursts that I wanted to eat.

As I began my journey through Candy Land I discovered some scrumptious trees with beautiful, mouthwatering, shiny red apples. I reached out and took a bite. *Crunch, crunch, crunch.* What a treat, sweet and tart and yummy to eat.

Above me were branches that tasted like lemons even though they were green. Below my feet, there was emerald wavy grass that tasted like lime and flowers that tasted sweet, divine and succulent.

As I stumbled along the wavy grass I saw on my right, there were towering, twisty and sticky candy canes that were as tall as a tower. Behind me were juicy, plump, heavy pumpkins that smelt like citrus fruits.

In the distance I came across a banana boat that smelt like a fluffy banana milkshake. I travelled on the boat through what appeared to be cotton candy clouds, down the silky smooth chocolate river, passing a waterfall that roared as it poured down the sugar-coated mountain until it landed into the raspberry rippled river.

As I climbed off the sweet banana boat I landed in a bed of monstrous, ruby-red mushrooms that tasted like strawberries and cream surrounded by enormous plants that tasted like plums, they were delectable.
Always remember, believe in your dreams and one day they may come true!
Amelia McDonald
Coit Primary School, Chapel Town

The Day I Saved Superman

Dear Diary,
This was the best day of my life because I got to meet Superman! This is what happened.
It was late on a Friday night in summer when my mum asked me to go to the bank to deposit the weekly takings. Reluctantly, I went. While I was stood in the queue two men dressed in black, wearing hats, scarves and sunglasses entered the bank holding guns. They were shouting, it was very confusing. The men demanded all of the bank's money and any jewellery the customers had. I felt scared, nervous and worried about everyone's safety.
While the robbers collected the jewellery in plastic bags, I heard a loud noise coming from above me. In the next moment, Superman came crashing through the roof to save the day. I felt a moment of relief and thought that we were going to be okay. But, it turned out the robbers had predicted Superman would turn up, so they came prepared with some kryptonite. This green stone stops Superman from using any of his powers. The robbers quickly tied him up and then went into the vaults to get the money.

When the robbers were out of sight, I suddenly felt brave. I crawled over to Superman, grabbed the kryptonite and threw it out of the window. A few moments later, Superman's powers returned and he gave me a wink and said thanks. I felt proud and a little shy.

By the time the robbers had cleared the vault, Superman was back to full strength and was waiting for them in the hallway. I could hear the robbers in the hallway laughing, but they were not laughing for long. They looked up to see Superman stood with his arms crossed ready to arrest them and send them to jail.

When everything was over, Superman came to see me and gave me a reward for my bravery and for helping him save the day!

Oliver James Haine (7)
Coit Primary School, Chapel Town

Boo And Me

Dear Diary,

Today I decided to go with Boo (my cat) on a camping adventure. She says the woods are the most fun place to be.

Boo helped me pack a bag so I would have everything I needed. A blanket to snuggle with. Some biscuits to munch on. A torch so I can see when it gets dark and some string for Boo, just in case she gets bored chasing squirrels.

We snuck out of the house and crept down to the woods just after tea. It was wonderful, Boo showed me all her favourite things. Bright coloured flowers with wonderful smells, spiders as big as my hand and all kinds of weird-looking bugs. Boo chased squirrels and butterflies and I hunted for pine cones until we were deep into the wood.

We found a stream running through the trees and Boo said it would be a lovely place to set up camp, so out came the blanket, biscuits and the ball of string (because Boo hadn't managed to catch any squirrels.)

Unfortunately, Boo had packed cat biscuits. Boo said, "They're very good." But I wasn't so sure so I decided to take a nap.

When I woke up, big fat raindrops had started to drip from the trees. The blanket started to get wet and cold. Boo was worried because I was too cold and I was coughing. She told me to follow her, she led me to a hollow tree. We climbed inside, it was lovely and dry but dark. I pulled the torch out of my bag and shined it high. Then Boo started to meow loudly. There was a noise outside the tree. I shined my torch outside and it was my parents. They had heard Boo's meows.

They took me and Boo home and dried us both off in front of the fire, with human biscuits for me and cat biscuits for Boo.

Oz Leonidas Edward Hiley (8)
Coit Primary School, Chapel Town

A Boy In The Amazon Rainforest

Dear Diary,
What a stressful and worrying week I have had. On Friday afternoon in the middle of my flight, the Captain was shouting stressfully. *Crash!* The plane hit the ground in the Amazon Rainforest and it shattered all over the emerald green trees that had a woody smell. Also, there were vines and they stood proud like soldiers.

Sadly, I still think all the other passengers died. The first thing I did was search the plane and I found clothing, little bits of food and a radio. Amazingly I found a den, it was made out of collapsed trees. I went in and all that was there were sharp faces dug into a tree. At least it was overgrown.

I felt anxious. In the distance, there was a greedy, hungry lion that had a soft mane. Later on, the same lion started looking at me. I had never been more scared! I was promised by the people that they would send help but they would arrive in three hours. So in that time I went to the Amazon River and got to the other side so the lion could not get me.

Now all I had to do was keep myself warm but that was hard with no blanket. The other thing I needed to do was keep myself well fed. The next morning my help arrived. Luckily I was in the perfect spot. The helicopter landed so I hopped on and that was the end of that. I was so glad to meet my lovely family again.

Zackary Round (8)
Coit Primary School, Chapel Town

The Time Machine Adventure

Dear Diary,
It was the craziest day of my life! It all started when we were in a peaceful park, Chad spotted a strange-looking object. Then I spotted a sign that said Keep us secret. We decided to go on it, but when we went inside Spot jumped in and before I knew it, it took off. That's when I suddenly realised that we were in a time machine!
Then, when we got out, we were in space! I was confused! Then Chad said, "What's that?" It was a sad-looking alien named Zog. We took him with us and travelled again. This time we went to Candyland. The ruler was a unicorn named Cookie. Cookie told us that their gem had been stolen by the evil witch. Zog wanted to come too but we told him it was too dangerous. We promised him that we would come back.
After we got out of the time machine we were surrounded by zombies. We went to the witch and she trapped us in a cage. She didn't know that the cage was full of keys. Spot began to bark when a door opened! Just before we left, we found the gem Cookie was talking about!

When we got into the time machine, we gave the gem to Cookie and said goodbye to everyone. We were back in the park. I hope you listened to my adventure but I must get to sleep. I hope you'll see me tomorrow.
Ocean

Totie Fong (7)
Coit Primary School, Chapel Town

The Day I Met Black Beard

Dear Diary,

I have had a brilliant day because I finally got to meet Captain Black Beard. So read on and I'll tell you all about it.

I called a taxi to have a ride to the harbour and the first thing I said was, "Wow, I have never seen a real pirate ship." But I wondered, *where is Captain Black Beard?*

Suddenly I heard someone shout, "Oscar!" It was Captain Black Beard. Then I gasped! He knew my name. It was the biggest surprise ever! "Oscar, will you join me on my ship?" questioned Captain Black, in wonder.

"Yes, of course I will." I was so excited.

"Alright, let's get going," shouted Captain Black Beard.

So then the ship set off. I nearly forgot to tell you, the ship was on its voyage. As we sailed on, the sea got rough so sadly some of the crew members tumbled off, but I didn't and neither did Captain Black Beard.

Then I felt something ticklish, it was the parrot. It was a very colourful parrot but also a very noisy parrot. Then Captian Black Beard shouted, "Land ahoy." We had been in a circle and we were back at the harbour.

"Woohoo, I loved that" I said.
So that was it, I loved that day!

Oscar Hudson (8)
Coit Primary School, Chapel Town

The Diary Of Ragnar The Explorer

Dear Diary,
Today was a very strange day. It all started quite normally, I decided to head down to the Jorvick Centre in York to learn about the vicious Vikings. All was going well until I found a peculiar object in the museum... I couldn't help but touch it. I kind of wish I didn't now. The room started spinning so fast, I thought I was going to be sick.
The next minute, I landed with a thud. I could feel the squelchy mud beneath my hands. I was far too terrified to open my eyes. I could hear fierce cries and the clashing of weapons. I remember feeling a rush of excitement rushing through me, but also feeling petrified at the same time.
When I finally built up the courage to open my eyes, I was shocked at the sight before me. Savage Viking warriors were dashing towards me, waving their swords like madmen! I'm not going to lie, I was panicking. I was pretty sure they could smell the fear.
I needed to get back to safety and I needed to get back sharpish.

Luckily for me, my one idea worked. I grabbed the time machine and got out of there and got home safely. Well, I won't be forgetting this day!
Ragnar.

Cole Michael Mullan (8)
Coit Primary School, Chapel Town

Tim

Dear Diary,

I was having a nice time in space. It was very peaceful up there, I had lots of time to think. When I first set off in my ruby-red rocket, I felt quite nervous. I couldn't believe I was going home soon. Maybe I wouldl take a walk on the moon just one more time.

Wait a minute, what is this mysterious creature hiding behind that crumbly ancient moon rock? I waited patiently to take a glance at the ancient creature. Suddenly the creature came from behind the rock.

The creature was emerald-green and furry, with only one eye and two blue antlers. The strange creature shuffled towards me and tried to talk to me but I didn't understand him. So instead, we used sign language.

The creature said his name was Blue and he was lost in space. The creature said, "Can I come with you Tim back to Earth?" He asked nicely.

Before me and Blue went back to Earth we played some games on the moon. Sadly, me and Blue had to go back to Earth, but I had a very good time there.

Lewis Mellors (7)
Coit Primary School, Chapel Town

The Incredible Diary Of Lucy

Dear Diary,
Today has been crazy and awesome. It all started at bedtime, it all went dark and I fell asleep. A second later, I had a dream that me and my cute dog, Roxy, were flying a kite in the fun, amazing park and the kite went higher and higher. I grabbed on to it and Roxy grabbed on to me and we went up into the clouds and we found a world that was different from ours. We had cupcakes and cake and there were roller coasters and an ice cream van that was open all week and all day. After about a five minute walk, we found a sign saying Boys' New World. It had superheroes, robots, and skateboards. We thought this was a boys and girls world. Thoughts raced around my head, *why is everybody the same?* I felt confused. Suddenly me and Roxy were falling out of the sky. Arghhhh!
I woke up feeling nervous. I was glad that wasn't real. *Bing! Bing!* My alarm went off and it was time for school. I told Mum and Dad about my dream.

Lucy Ball (8)
Coit Primary School, Chapel Town

The Incredible Diary Of...

Dear Diary,
Today I was put on to a colossal black ship called the Titanic, but before I got on the Titanic I noticed a black bump on the end of the ship. The next thing I knew I was on the bottom floor.

A couple of hours went past and an alarm went off. I knew it was because there were icebergs near. An hour passed and then *bump!* The ship had hit something. I knew it was the iceberg. I was petrified. Then a speech came on and it said we were going to sink. I was sad.

Then I was on the Captain's floor and I was suffocating, I had about ten seconds left but the sea water was nearly at me. Nine seconds left, and then it got to me. I swam to the bottom of the ship and saw an escaping bit. I didn't get to it in time but I saw another door that was open, so I was free.

When I got out, the ship was fully under the sea. I was sad. Then I went back to my home of fish and I told them about it. Free at last.

Spencer Mounsey (8)
Coit Primary School, Chapel Town

Captain Purplebeard

Dear Diary,

Today has been the most frustrating day of my *entire* life, I'll tell you all about it.

At the start of the morning, the shine of my treasures hit my brain. Thoughts raced around my head, should I go again? My heart said yes but my brain said no. *Always follow your heart* I thought. When I went out a rumour went around that a pile of all valuables was on an island. As dumb as I am, I fell for it and booted up The Old Jolly Roger (my pirate ship).

I didn't invite anyone else because I wanted it all for myself. Pointless hours of nothing, it was so far away. It was like to the South Pole and back in exactly thirteen hours, fifteen minutes and thirteen seconds. When I arrived, I threw the map into the water because I found that it was fake. Me and my ship had to go all the way back.

I'm tired. Sorry, I need to go to bed now. I hope you can listen to the story tomorrow.

Sriyan Sen (7)
Coit Primary School, Chapel Town

The Show

Dear Diary,

On the 3rd of April, 2017, me and my best friends went and did two dances. We danced to True Colours from Trolls for the first dance and Black Magic for the second dance. We ate a few snacks in the interval and then we did our second dance. After that, I ate a chocolate bar and my friends ate one too.

After the show, we went to Olivia's house for tea and to Daisy's house to play. We had lots of fun there, so we went to my house for a sleepover. The next day we had to do another show but we went on holiday afterwards.

We had lots more fun when we finished the finale, because we all won a dancing trophy and gymnastics trophy for all of the hard work that we had done on the stage, and backstage as well. We looked after the babies in the baby room and helped them put on their outfits and clothes.

Lucy Iris Sykes (8)
Coit Primary School, Chapel Town

Life

Dear Diary,

Today was an emotional day because I had a flypast in Endcliffe Park to remember the crash that happened seventy-five years ago when I was eight.

I got to stand on a huge stage in front of thousands of people and tell my story on television.

Then at 8:45am the flypast happened which involved ten American military aircraft flying over the park. As the aircraft flew over, the crowd started to cheer. I looked up at the planes and waved. I had mixed emotions because I was proud of the flypast but I was also sad as I remembered those ten US airmen that died seventy-five years ago.

At the end of the day, I hope those ten airmen were looking down and were really proud of what happened today.

Tony.

Olivia Rose Batty (8)
Coit Primary School, Chapel Town

Scarlet's Big Race

Dear Diary,
Today I am writing about the amazing day I had. First, I got in my group then I went over to the throwing area. I waited for my turn and then I took my turn (it took a long time to do another activity). Next, I did the standing long jump but I don't think I was very good at it. Then I waited a long time until I could do my two-lap adventure. It was my turn but the sad news was I came last.
Finally, it was my last race, the 60-metre run. When the gun went I was off and I didn't come last, I came fourth.
Last but not least, I got a certificate and some people got a medal but I didn't get a medal but it's the taking part that matters.

Scarlet Boothby (8)
Coit Primary School, Chapel Town

Help!

Dear Diary,
Today was the worst day of my life. I was sailing down the Atlantic Ocean when pirates attacked my ship and took it away. I was thrown overboard and left to swim to shore.
I swam all night and finally found a desert island. Now, how do I survive? Where will I find food and shelter?

Dear Diary,
Day three. I found coconuts and bananas to eat and I made a shelter out of palm leaves and twigs.

Dear Diary,
Day four. I found some big stones and spelt HELP in the sand with them.

Dear Diary,
It had been a few weeks and I started to like it on the island. Then I got rescued by a helicopter and got home.

Olly Gillott (8)
Coit Primary School, Chapel Town

The Diary Of Oliver

Dear Diary,
Today has been the best day because I woke up in Ibiza. I jumped out of bed and got dressed in my comfy clothes.
Then I went downstairs and had a full English, it tasted beautiful and I felt like I could've had another one. Excitedly, I went into my neat and tidy room. I got my swimming shorts out because I was going to go to the swimming pool.
Tiredly, I went to my room to sleep and after that, I had delicious food. Then I watched a film.
This was the best day of my life.

Oliver Colville (7)
Coit Primary School, Chapel Town

All About My Shopping Spree!

Dear Diary,

Today I went to Meadowhall and I went to Claire's to get some glasses. Then I went to the jewellers. I chose a gold ring that I loved. Then I went to Frankie and Benny's for lunch. I had three burgers and mash potato with corn on the cob. For dessert, I had a brownie and ice cream which was so delicious. I also had two milkshakes. I was really full.

Then I went clothes shopping and then I went to The Body Shop to get my auntie some stuff. After, I caught a taxi home.

Kayla Davis (7)
Coit Primary School, Chapel Town

A Day At The Zoo!

Dear Diary

Today I went to the zoo, it was one of the best days ever. I went to the ticket office and the queue was huge. After getting my ticket I walked through to the first part of the zoo. I saw a really big strong elephant. Its trunk was long and it used it to suck up all the water. It would then spray the water all over himself.

The next part of the zoo had an alligator, it had spikes on its back. The alligator had a very long body. I even saw the alligator feeding.

Owen Lever (8)
Coit Primary School, Chapel Town

Harvey's Outstanding Day

Dear Diary,

Today I went to space, but on the way, there was an enormous incident. The spaceship's ancient, old engine went funny and we had to go back to Earth to see what the incident was. So we went back and we had to put more ashy, gassy petrol in. Then we went into space because the engine was fine. We saw googly aliens with their bodies upside down.

Harvey Poulter (8)
Coit Primary School, Chapel Town

A Day In The Life Of School Shoes

Dear Diary,
Good morning, at the moment it is 6:35am. This is usually the time my owner wakes up. My owner's name is Amelia Grace Cook, also known as Cookie. At the moment I feel really wretched because I have a huge cavity in my sole. I am struggling to open my eyes and focus on the busy day ahead. Due to these issues I face on a daily basis, I am expected to cover a huge number of miles. Some people treat me unfairly and say that I smell. I have an amazing relationship with my owner due to the amount of time we have spent together over the years.

As the sun rises it is time that my jam-packed day will start. However, I am still not that awake. Amelia is coming. Soon I will be awake starting my journey filled with excitement. "Oww!" This is the worst part of my day, Amelia has to put me on. Don't tell her I said this, but she has really broad, fat feet, no offence.

She looked down at me and said, "None taken."
"Oops! I think she heard me!"

Yay! It's time to go. I can't wait for today we have PE with Amelia's teacher, Mr Cartwright. My favourite part of the day except for break and lunch. Around one hour has passed, we have boring English and RE. Oh yeah, I have just remembered it's PE time. Amelia needs to get changed. Now it's football, yes! Amelia is going in for the tackle. "Ouch!" I think Amelia has broken her ankle. It's off to hospital for us. Looks like I'm going to be bored for a long time. We're just being rushed to the bones department for an X-ray. Half an hour has passed and unfortunately, it is broken and will be in a moon boot for six weeks. Plus no football, how bored I'm going to be!

Amelia Cook (10)
Greasbrough Primary School, Greasbrough

Noodling On Lake Lewisville
An extract

Friday 29th March, 2019. Lake Lewisville, Texas.
Dear Diary,
The time is 8am. Today I am very excited because I am looking for the Oklahoma flathead catfish. After a quick breakfast, I was off. I travelled sixty miles by Jeep and reached Lake Lewisville. I have boarded the airboat for the shallow water near the bank of the lake. The crafty catfish should be under the lake. With me today are Levi and Western who are experts at noodling (the art of catching fish with bare hands).

Dear Diary,
The time is now 9:30am. We reached the banks of the lake and Western dove off the boat and spotted some large holes along the bank. He quietly showed a thumb out of the lake to let us know we were in luck and just might noodle the predator that I'd been looking for. I quietly slipped into the water beside Western. Levi stayed in the boat. I took the first hole and blocked the entrance, Western took the second entrance.

Suddenly, with a mighty splash, a water snake jumped up and went for my arm. Levi knocked it away from me with a paddle.

On our second attempt, Levi got out of the boat and we blocked each of the three entrances. I took a deep breath and dived under the water. I put my hand into the hole. I felt for the catfish's mouth and put my hand at the top to avoid being cut by the long, thin, sharp spines. After twenty minutes of fighting with the catfish, I pulled it out and we wrestled with it while it tried to outwit us with a death roll. We held on like limpets to a rock and we pulled it onto the boat.

Levi weighed the monster, a whopping ninety-seven pounds. A world record! We gently put it back into the water, but not before I gave it a kiss. This was one of the best days of my life.

George Lee Henderson (8)
Greasbrough Primary School, Greasbrough

Always

An extract

Dear Diary,

Today started like any other day. I woke up hearing my mum come down the stairs. I said, "Hello," and she gave me lots of love and a good stroke by my ears. She knows how much I like that. Then I went outside like normal. I sniffed around making sure the garden was all clear before I went to the toilet. It was quite cold this morning so I did not want to stay outside for long, also I could not wait any longer to see Kara and Cole. They are always fun to play with and Kara gives me extra treats when Mummy is not looking.

So off inside I went, straight upstairs to Kara's room where I jumped on her bed. I always put my hand near Kara's head and nudge her until she wakes up. It did not take long until she opened her eyes and smiled at me.

We both ran to jump on Cole's bed. I licked him as he put his arms around my neck.

I ran down the stairs, looking at Mummy in the kitchen. She had done my breakfast, yummy. As Kara and Cole were getting ready for school I stayed by them, following them when they moved. I hated when they went to school, Mummy is fun but not as fun as Kara and Cole.

Mummy took me for a walk to the park. I ran around chasing the ball and seeing other dogs. Some were friendly and some just barked at me. We came home and I fell asleep, my Mom tidied up. Hopefully it would not be long until school finished.

Yay! 3pm came, Kara and Cole would be home soon. Mummy had gone to pick them up. I waited by the door so that I could see them straight away. As soon as they got home we played ball and running, lots of running.

Kara May Bentley (7)
Greasbrough Primary School, Greasbrough

Me And My Idol

Dear Diary,

This week was the worst week of my life! On Monday, I noticed posters placed around school asking for pupils to audition for the school play. School auditions took place in the assembly hall and I had auditioned for a singing part. When I stood up on stage, I felt just like a star, like Taylor Swift. But as soon as I started to sing, I ran off with stage fright. I asked Miss if I could try again at lunch.

Dear Diary,

I got it, I got the part! Everybody was crowding around me after school and people were asking me to sing. I started to sing and walk around but all of a sudden, *bang!* I tripped over a tree stump. I was so embarrassed! Everyone was laughing. I ran to my house as quick as I could, hoping that no one would mention it at school.

Dear Diary,

On Tuesday, no one uttered a word about what happened.

Dear Diary,

Nothing really happened on Tuesday, Wednesday or Thursday, it was the same old boring day.

Today, on Friday, it was the day of the play. I was so nervous.

When it got to my part, I stood up in front of all the grown-ups and collapsed on the stage!

My mum called an ambulance and here I am now, sitting in a hospital bed with manky food and smelly nurses.

But in the end, I've learnt that people make mistakes, even Taylor Swift, and sometimes it's a good thing because you can improve on your mistakes and try again.

I will write soon.

Leah Joanne Hardwick (10)
Greasbrough Primary School, Greasbrough

Secret Life Of My Dogs

Dear Diary,
It's that time again when I can hear footsteps. I am excited. I love it when Libby gets up. She always comes for a cuddle and opens the door and we can smell that lovely morning fresh air. Libby always has tea and biscuits for breakfast and we always get a treat from her. What we don't like is when we see her put her school coat on and bag. This can only mean one thing, she is leaving for school. It makes me feel sad and lonely.

While she's away the house is quiet and boring. It makes me feel tired waiting for her to come home so I look around the house for things to do or play with. I like taking all the cushions off the sofa and emptying the toy box. I also like opening drawers and taking socks but Libby's mum said I shouldn't do any of that. Even though I do most days, or every day.

Then after hours of looking through the window and barking at everything, even our own shadows, we can hear the sound of the car. Libby runs up the garden shouting our names, "Milly, Penny!" I get excited. Yes, she's home. I love her.

Where is my ball? Let's play ball. Libby and her sister, Molly, play ball with us for ages. But sometimes Molly is too lazy so Libby will just play. Libby will play for hours until she goes up for a bath and tea.

After Libby has had her bath we all cuddle up on the sofa and watch TV. I love cuddles.

Libby Exley (9)
Greasbrough Primary School, Greasbrough

Nemo!

Dear Diary,

Today I was swimming to school. While I was swimming I could see shoals of colourful fish waddling their fins across the ocean. I could see the coral reef dancing as the ocean water brushed softly against it. Starfish lay silently on stacked up rocks while I saw a little sea turtle family glide past me!

After I admired everything around me I normally carried on swimming... In a blink of an eye, two ferocious-looking divers appeared in front of me! I froze in shock, not knowing what to do! As soon as I saw those divers I really should have swum for my life...

As quick as a flash, one of the divers disappeared but the other one had this weird gadget that made this clicking noise and made a big flash. Everything went black for a few seconds...

After that happened, I was at the surface of the ocean! I soon realised I was in this tiny net, but then I was out of the water. I started to panic, thinking, *will I die? Will I ever see my daddy again?*

Next thing I knew I was at the side of a huge boat. I thought to myself, *those silly divers put me at the edge of the boat!* "Ha, I need to flop off the boat!" I said struggling to breathe.
I jumped with all my might and *plop!* I was where I belonged, in the ocean.

Nell White (10)
Greasbrough Primary School, Greasbrough

The Adventures Of Zoltar The Dog

Dear Diary,

Today, I travelled to a parallel world where everything was the opposite. It was very strange. When I got there, I met myself, but opposite. In there, I was stupid and I didn't know how to walk. I investigated some more and was suddenly captured by Cybermen. I woke up in a machine where I was ready to become a Cyberman. Suddenly, I jumped out and immediately did a homing attack on every Cyberman and did a very dramatic pose with explosions.

I travelled back to my own world and got into my TARDIS which stands for Time And Relative Dimensions In Space or, if you prefer, Totally A-Radical Driving In Space.

Then, I did a mystery trip. I arrived at an old amusement park where there was a giant slide that had been shut down because Daleks had taken over. By the way, I'm a time dog. The Daleks hadn't noticed me yet, so I snuck around the back. Meanwhile... "TARDIS located, Zoltar located, Zoltar is located!" The Daleks searched for me so, for fun, I jumped into the range of the Daleks. "Exterminate!"

At that moment, I spun onto the crossfire and shouted, "Chao's control!" and, with a very cool word, I exterminated the Daleks.
In the end, I went on the giant waterslide and I had an amazing time!

Jack Portman (9)
Greasbrough Primary School, Greasbrough

Jake The Pug Gets Lost

Dear Diary,
You'll never guess what happened to me the other day! It was so scary, I've got to tell you about it! It was a cold winter's evening on the 7th of November. I was playing catch with my owner when the ball rolled out of the garden! I went to fetch the ball, it rolled into the street. My owner shouted me back but I felt safe and saw lots of trees ahead.

Excitement set in and I ran towards the trees where I'd been many times before on walks with my family. I went into the forest looking for adventure and chasing bugs, which led me deeper into the forest. I looked around. I didn't know which way to go home. I started to shake with fear, I'd never been alone before. I started to feel cold and hungry. I whimpered while listening to weird noises around me. I heard a ribbit sound coming from a rock. I jumped as a frog leapt out and stared at me.

As I followed it, not knowing where I was going, I kept up with the frog. All of a sudden there started to be more daylight. I suddenly realised I was where I started!

Across the street, my home and family stood shouting my name. I ran over to them and jumped right into their arms. I was so happy.

Selina Royala Smith (8)
Greasbrough Primary School, Greasbrough

Friendship

Dear Diary,

I was really sad today because my best friends don't like me anymore. The new girl, Ella, doesn't know this school yet so my friends are always trying to get Ella's attention. I have been trying and trying to get her attention to show them that I am their best friend. They don't listen to me, they tell me to go away or say, "You can't tell us." Sometimes they say stop it, Madi goes and plays with someone else or goes to miss for a bit. But I didn't listen to my friends I moved on and my new best friends are Emme and Lola because the same thing happened to them.

Now I can have someone to trust and someone to help me. Now they're jealous and sad like I was, they can feel the pain and how much it hurt me. Now they've moved on. I think this because they always walk past me laughing and telling jokes. I think they just do this to make me jealous because I made new friends before they did.

Oh sorry, got to go now because my dinner is ready. See you soon, I can't wait to see what happens tomorrow, I heard our teacher has a fun day planned for us. Hopefully, that will cheer me up.

Madison Willers (9)
Greasbrough Primary School, Greasbrough

The Catastrophe

Dear Diary,
I was taken to Haven by my owner Ava. As I sat in the car with her, I felt so excited to be going to the seaside. We got to the caravan which was huge and spacious. We got changed and went to see the characters at the show bar. I danced with Ava to Baby Shark and she was swinging me around, it made me dizzy.

Dear Diary,
Today we went swimming, the water was crystal-clear and warm. I watched Ava with Ava's mum. Afterwards, we went to the arcade and she held me tight.
Suddenly I found myself alone. I was scared, lonely and worried. I went to a security guard and said, "I've lost my owner, will you help me?"
"What does your owner look like?"
I described Ava. "She has long blonde hair, big blue eyes and she is wearing a denim dress."
"Is that her?"
I was so relieved, there was Ava and her family. The security guard waved at Ava and she ran and scooped me up. I had never been so happy and I will never wander off again.

Ava Jessica Frier (8)
Greasbrough Primary School, Greasbrough

Rolo's Adventure

Dear Diary,
Today has been the best day ever! Early in the morning, my owner was about to go to work but she left her bag and had to come back for it. I saw from the corner of my eye a bright light. It was coming through the door from outside, the door had been left open. This was my chance, I made a run for it. As I got outside the sun was shining, but I got frightened because the leaves were moving on their own. In the distance, I heard a robin, it was red and brown. It was tweeting in the trees. So I jumped on the fence and I started to chase the beautiful robin.

When I lost the robin, I was excited because I ended up in this weird place called the park. There were happy children playing but when I walked past them they looked at me like they were going to chase me. Finally, they caught me but another cat came out of nowhere and jumped on the children. The cat looked like a tiger cat and he saved me. When I was about to say thank you, my owner grabbed me and took me home. I was sad to go, but I was happy to be back home.

Kayla McErlean (8)
Greasbrough Primary School, Greasbrough

The Diary Of Dance

Dear Diary,
Today I finally got in an actual dance studio! My mum called and they let me join. I'm pretty nervous because I start tomorrow, tomorrow is Wednesday.

Dear Diary,
Today it is Wednesday. After school, I got to dance but now I'm even more nervous. I got scared while I was at dance, the dance teacher is so kind. I'm scared to make new friends though.

Dear Diary,
Today is my second time going, it's the next Wednesday again. I'm scared to make new friends.

Dear Diary,
It is my third Wednesday here and I'm so excited because I finally made a friend! I feel so excited.

Dear Diary,
It is now my fourth Wednesday here and now I am best friends with her. When we eat dinner we always sit with each other. Now I am friends with everybody who dances here! I should have believed in myself.

I'm super impressed and I can't wait for next Wednesday. Now I have started dancing three times a week and I feel like a professional dancer!

Megan Lily Wright (8)
Greasbrough Primary School, Greasbrough

Princess Sparkles

Dear Diary,
Today was the most action-packed day. I was making fairy cakes to attract luck fairies to grant me three wishes. When I went outside to get a daisy, the sky fell dark so I knew something was up. A shadow hung above me. I picked the daisy and tried to run inside, but I dropped it and two legs grabbed me by the wings. I tried to wriggle out, but it felt like falling upwards. It gripped tighter. It was the terrifying Gloom Dragon! I felt shocked. Was I going for a friendly visit, or to end up as supper?
At last, we arrived at the unhappy cave. It was dark and echoey. A faint snoring noise filled the cave. We arrived at a section of the cave where there was a male dragon curled up beside a baby dragon which was fast asleep. I was scared of what could happen. All of a sudden, I heard the clopping of hooves. It was the handsome, brave Prince Chester. He shot an arrow at the Gloom Dragon and grabbed my horn while the Gloom Dragon was distracted. We flew home and Prince Chester asked me to marry him. I accepted!

Sophia Barlow (8)
Greasbrough Primary School, Greasbrough

Wentworth Park

Dear Diary,
Today we went to the park. We got lost in the park's labyrinth and we climbed up a hill. Then we saw my dad and my brother. My dad told my mum where she had to go. After that, we saw a pheasant in the garden. The pheasant got scared and ran away. Different types of flowers made the garden so beautiful. There was a river, people put some coins in the river.
Next, we went near the gazelles. We watched them a little bit and then we went to a picnic place. We had a picnic. We made a race, throwing stones into the pond with my brother. We enjoyed it. We went to the pet shop and saw fish, hamsters and rabbits. From there we went to the playground, it was the first time I swung on my own. We went to the lake by our car but the weather was so windy, we changed our plan and returned home. We had a lot of fun.
When we came back to our house my dad asked me, "How can you stand like that?"
I said, "Because I am a child, of course I can!"

Zeynep Beyza Sargin (8)
Greasbrough Primary School, Greasbrough

A Professional Footballer

Dear Diary,
Today was the day! My alarm went off at 6am although I didn't need it because I was already awake from nerves. I had to turn my nerves into strength because today was going to be the biggest match in my football career! I got my kit bag ready with my football boots and training kit in. Before I knew it I was on my way to Anfield Football Ground.

When I got there it was time to go into my team's (Liverpool) changing room. There it was, my kit shining like the bright sun. It was like no one else's kit was there. Then my manager shouted me out, it was time for training half hour before the cup final. After training, we went into the changing rooms and got our football kit on. I was really nervous but excited at the same time.

There I was stood in the tunnel waiting to go out on the pitch. The whistle blew! It was my time. The match began and in the first ten minutes, I scored! I'm so proud of myself, I wonder what will happen next.

Heidi Florence Astle (10)
Greasbrough Primary School, Greasbrough

The Best Footballer In The World

Dear Diary,

It was my first time playing for Real Madrid and we were winning two-nil at half time. I was shocked because I took a shot and it hit the crossbar and went in. After half time, Bayern Munich scored two goals and it was Lewoski. I was shocked because I thought *how has Lewoski scored ten minutes after half time?* I scored again, it was in top bins. I was excited because we could win the quarter-finals. Then I crossed it and Gareth Bale did an overhead kick and it went in the back of the net. We were winning the quarter-finals. Then in two minutes, Lewoski scored again but after that, the whistle blew and I won the quarter-finals.

Then we won the semi-finals and the final. We got a gold medal and trophy to go in Real Madrid's cabinet. It was silver and gold, it was beautiful. I was in the Champions League and I got signed to Juventus. It cost 200,000 pounds to buy me.

Dylan James Currie (7)
Greasbrough Primary School, Greasbrough

A Pregnant Mum

Dear Diary,
I ran downstairs to grab my pencil to write in this diary. It's 8am on a Saturday morning. I can hear puking noises coming from the toilet. Is Mummy alright? I can hear her asking for her mum. Daddy runs upstairs with a glass of water for my mum. I can't look at that glass anymore. I wish she would hurry up in the toilet because I really need to pee.

Dear Diary,
Nothing unusual happened until 3pm, Daddy is currently tormenting Mummy. He keeps sniffing her and he's just told her she smells of poop. Now Mummy is crying her eyeballs out. Why is she crying all of the time?

Dear Diary,
It is 7:30pm and none of us can go to the toilet because Mummy is pooping yet again. Daddy was explaining that we might have to be at one with nature like Bear Grylls. Then Mummy stopped him talking so I don't know what he meant.

Jack Clay (7)
Greasbrough Primary School, Greasbrough

The Imaginary Adventure

Dear Diary,

Yesterday me and my cousin went on an adventure, but it was all in Bobbie's brain. Bobbie is my cousin. It was amazing. We went to the park and that is when it started. Me and Bobbie were on a wacky adventure, we got lost in the sea. Bobbie and I can't swim so there was a little boat. I picked Bobbie up and put her on the boat. I climbed on it. We ended up on a beach, me and Bobbie were so shocked.

In five minutes we saw a mermaid. We spoke to the mermaid for a while, then we set off looking for where to go next. Then we went to sleep on the beach. We forgot we did so we were scared.

In a cave the next day we saw a humongous octopus. It was purple and had black spots, we were excited. After all the excitement, me and Bobbie were ready for another wacky, fun adventure. And that was the end. Be ready for another adventure.

Imogen Ashcroft (8)
Greasbrough Primary School, Greasbrough

Who's Done It?

Dear Diary,
On Sunday me and my sister Evie were playing upstairs. Daddy was at work and Mummy was cooking dinner. Suddenly Mummy shouted, "Have you been leaving Fruit Shoot bottles outside?" She sounded cross.
Me and Evie shook our heads and said, "No."
"Okay,' said Mummy.
We went back upstairs. Mummy heard a noise outside. When Mummy got to the door, she couldn't believe what she saw, our boxer dog, Bella. She had her nose in the bag of Fruit Shoots. Mummy quickly got her phone to record it, she got her on video. Bella was using her paws to get herself a drink. She picked one up with her mouth and ran off as quick as a flash down the garden. Mummy knew who to blame, me and Evie didn't get told off. We laughed and laughed when we watched the video on Mummy's phone.

Jake Elliott (8)
Greasbrough Primary School, Greasbrough

Ariana Grande's Microphone

Dear Diary,

I woke up bright and early. Ariana put me in my case and the next thing I knew, I was already in the car to the airport.

I woke up a few hours later to the classical music in the first-class lounge. There I was, put beside Ariana Grande in a shuttle case.

The next thing I knew, I heard the captain say that we were about to land, so I held on tight to the foam sides inside the case, then I waited and waited and waited. Suddenly, the case was opened by one of the crew from backstage.

When they got me out, I was in a dark room with flashing lights above me. At first, the light kind of blinded me but when I was put on the mic stand, I was able to see where I was. I was on the stage! I heard footsteps on the stage. Then out of nowhere appeared Ariana Grande. I heard the music start and she started singing.

Anna Sofia Kurti (9)
Greasbrough Primary School, Greasbrough

The Never-Ending Journey

Dear Diary,

Today I was watching gymnastics, then my friend called and said I should come to her house. When I got there, she came to me on the beach. My friend is a mermaid. If you think that's crazy, well I'm a fairy.

Then we went underwater, then we played some computer games. You could not do that normally but these games are magic. Then once we had done all the levels we got snapped into the game. It was like magic.

Then we asked an owl how we got here, he said, "Something is wrong with the power source!" So we started to make our way to the power source. We crossed a tangly jungle, crashing seas and a pixie hollow.

Then finally we made it. I recharged it with my magic, then we were whisked home back to my friend's house. I don't want to play that computer game again!

Megan Evison (8)
Greasbrough Primary School, Greasbrough

Bonnie's Adventure

Dear Diary,
Today I was so excited to go for a walk to the field where I always go with my owner, Graham. We set off at about 4:30pm like normal and it just felt like any other day. I had no idea what was going to happen. We got to the field and Graham threw the ball like he always does. This time when I went to catch it I ran into the fence and got my head stuck! I opened my eyes and saw a massive bull running towards me in the farmer's field next door. I was scared and Graham looked very worried. Graham shouted at the farmer to stop the bull, and then he ran to the bull to stop it. I was so relieved when the bull stopped running and went back to the farmer. Graham helped me out of the fence and took me home.
I had some tea and now I'm so tired after my adventure I am going to go to bed.

Arran Curran (8)
Greasbrough Primary School, Greasbrough

Lost In The Rainforest

Dear Diary,
I am in a little town in my bedroom staring out of the window watching people walk by. My dad and I bought a ticket to go on a plane to Malaysia but we have to cross the rainforest. I am scared of the animals in the rainforest. It is time to go on the plane. We are on the plane right now and are setting off.

Dear Diary,
Two hours later I am still on the plane, but one minute later I hear a big bang! I look out of the window and the plane is crashing.
When I wake up my dad is next to me with a big bruise like me. My dad and I are the only ones who survived. I think, *where am I?* Then I start to get hungry and thirsty. When I hear a plane I wave and they come to get me and my dad and take me back to my small town.

Lily May Williams (9)
Greasbrough Primary School, Greasbrough

The Adventures Of Freddie

Dear Diary,
Today I went to the music stadium to see the greatest band, Little Mix. They were awesome! My favourite band, Queen, came up to me with all the instruments and said, "Yo, Freddie. We need a new band member, we would love for it to be you!" This was the most surprising thing that has ever happened to me! So they took me to their practice room, which had lights, cameras and drums. I had a go at playing them all, I wasn't very good so I played the flute but in-between practices, they taught me to play air guitar. I did! We went wild. I finally went to the stage and played in front of hundreds, maybe even thousands. We had the greatest time of our lives.

Eva Natasha Sanderson (9)
Greasbrough Primary School, Greasbrough

Dane The Dog!

Dear Diary,

I woke up this morning from my doggy nap and started to woof woof! I was very hungry. I went over to my bowl and ate everything, yummy, and now I am full. When I finished I ran to my owner to lick him on his cheek. I saw him getting his coat on and he got my lead. I was so excited I was wagging my tail until he put my lead on and we went for a walk.

When we were on a walk we saw a dog adoption centre. We went inside and picked a new doggy for me to be friends with.

We then went home and I played with my new dog friend. We shared toys, food and my bed. We got so tired from playing all night long, we went to bed with tired doggy minds. Woof! Night night. Woof!

Olivia Craven (8)
Greasbrough Primary School, Greasbrough

Ninja

Dear Diary,
Today I have witnessed the most amazing thing in the world. Oh, by the way, I'm a keyboard. Anyway, you won't believe what happened. My owner, Ninja (Tyler Blevins), got a victory today on Fortnite Battle Royale, so here's what happened.
He was playing solo and found something mysterious, something that would change his life. It was a mysterious gun that could shoot out energy balls that could destroy anything, including Fortnite characters! He used it. He kept on winning and winning, he was unstoppable. He had over 1,000,000 wins and became the most known streamer in the world for what he did!

Reece Cobi Hazelhurst (10)
Greasbrough Primary School, Greasbrough

Me Wanting To Make A Kit

Dear Diary,

On Monday I asked my mum, "Can I have a football kit?"

"No," my mum said.

"Why not?"

"Because it is too much money."

"No, it is only fifty pounds."

"Why would you want to buy one anyway?"

"Because I've always dreamed of building my own football team and beating Manchester United with them."

On Tuesday my mum handed me fifty pounds and said, "You can build your own football team." She is the best mum ever.

Anthony Peter Roddis (11)
Greasbrough Primary School, Greasbrough

Princess Beatrice's Coronation

Dear Diary,
This will be the most exciting day of my life. I will be crowned Queen which is so special for me. Even my mother, Sarah Duchess of York, made it. She is extremely proud.

As I was travelling in a black, shiny car, butterflies started floating around my stomach as I did not know what was going to happen. As soon as I stepped on to the cobbled steps, my worries began to vanish away because I knew that everything would go right. The moment I was crowned Queen Beatrice my life was complete. I have the opportunity to make this world right and no one will regret it.

Beatrice Bradley (10)
Greasbrough Primary School, Greasbrough

Freddie Mercury And His Mind-Blowing Diary

Dear Diary,
Today I went on stage to a big crowd. My heart was beating really fast like fireworks ready to start. They were all singing back to me and shouting my name. I felt like I was loved. I was sweating like no other. It was the second song and I was kinda getting used to it. I was gobsmacked how much people loved me. I mean, I am a legend after all, right? It was the best day of my life!

Yazmin Dewick (9)
Greasbrough Primary School, Greasbrough

Once Upon A Time

Dear Diary,

Today I, the Saviour, became the chief and I helped everybody stay safe while Regina, the evil queen, tried to take everybody's hearts. Elsa also came and marshmallows had been made by my parents, Snow White and Prince Charming, with my brother Prince Nile. I defeated all the bad guys except Captain Hook. I pulled out my gun and *boom!* I defeated him.

Ella Rose Williams (9)
Greasbrough Primary School, Greasbrough

Egypt

Dear Diary,
Today was the best day of my life, I became king. I am the youngest king that ever lived. They woke me up and told me about the fabulous day I would have. I started off with a palace, then slaves, then a crown, then a staff and then untold riches. We had a grand feast to celebrate my day.

Tristan Allan (10)
Greasbrough Primary School, Greasbrough

The Incredible Diary Of...

Dear Diary,
I was walking with my dog when I found a black and white cat on his own. He began to follow me. I called him Felix. I took Felix home with me and gave him a loving home.

Darcey Flint (7)
Greasbrough Primary School, Greasbrough

My Dog Diary
An extract

Dear Diary

Today was amazing! It was the best day ever! Shall I tell you what happened? I got adopted by a lovely couple! Let me tell you from the beginning.

This morning, I woke up and stretched my paws as far as they would go and I wagged my short, fluffy tail. As I started to run around, one of the workers came in and in a happy voice, she shouted, "Breakfast!" All I could hear were all the other crazy dogs barking. Finally, it was my turn to have my food. It was beef biscuits, my favourite! After that, random people came rushing in to find a beloved pet.

Walking towards me was a fantastic-looking couple who even had a daughter. The small girl ran towards me and yelled, "This one!"

I felt nervous but excited to be free and have a family. The shelter owner opened my locked door and let me go. I ran straight into the girl's arms. I licked her all around her face and started jumping all about. When they took me outside, we went straight to buy a collar which would be my first one with my new home on it. "I'm going to call you Lucy!" the girl said. "I'm called Chloe!" After the collar was made, she put it straight on me.

This was my favourite bit, going to the park. As we walked, I kept on running around the family non-stop. When I explored the outside world, I could smell the fragrance of out-of-date hot dogs. Lying on the floor was a rotten hot dog. I opened my mouth to try the new food when Chloe knelt down and threw a stick. I looked up, waiting for her to say 'fetch' and, guess what? She did! After half an hour, we went back to my new wonderful home.

Zainab Ul-Hassan (10)
Hatchell Wood Primary Academy, Bessacarr

The Incredible Diary Of...

Dear Diary,

Today, a surprising thing happened. I woke up expecting another normal day of waiting for a family to buy me, when a towering lady picked me up! "What on Earth?" I asked my family below me. I was on level with the lady now; she had a kind face and looked quite young. She then passed me to a small girl next to her. She too looked kind.

Ahh, this is the life! I thought as the girl stroked me gently. Then, she announced something I thought would never happen. "He's the one! I'll take him!" Before I knew it, I was put in a carry case and my family was blocked from view. Not long after my departure, I was in a snuggly, warm house full of hay, food and a blue, fluffy bed inside a lovely, blue box. It was the best!

Later on, the girl who had picked me up came to me; as she approached, I felt a little scared but I didn't need to worry. She petted me and hugged me and said her name was Mille and that mine would me... (ready? It's so cute!) Midnight! I loved it! After the most wonderful snuggle, she let me out to explore their perfectly mown garden; the grass was delicious and the greenhouse was warm - was that right?

As evening drew near, Millie and her mum, Joanne, came and gathered up my stuff. After a while, I was carried towards their living room. As we entered, my stuff was on the floor! I loved my owners!
Well, good night! I'll write again soon!
Midnight, signing off.

Millie Taylor (10)
Hatchell Wood Primary Academy, Bessacarr

The Catastrophic Diary Of Mitzy

27th July, 2018
Dear Diary,
Today was an interesting day. I woke up at 5am. I was extremely tired. I could barely stand, but I didn't want to miss the day. I wandered around for hours, waiting for my family to wake up. Eventually, I get bored and headbutted the shorter one until he got up. Then, I moved onto my mother, I woke her up by stepping on her. She seemed to be in pain for some reason. I don't understand humans.
After that, I went back to the child, who was in the room that my dad went in before he left, and stepped on his leg to get his attention. He wasn't in pain. Makes you wonder, are humans born equally? Then came my favourite time of the day: food time! Today, I got a choice of Dreamies or Asda cat food. Of course, I picked the superior one: Asda cat food. As normal, I went for my midday nap. I felt like the family didn't like me sleeping, but I can't stop sleeping, I'm addicted.
A few hours later, I was woken by a knocking on the door. I walked downstairs to see what was happening. To my surprise, I saw some kids and, to make it worse, they came in.

Were my cat eyes deceiving me? At first, I was okay, but more and more kids were rolling in. Before long, the whole estate was here! At this point, I was really upset so I decided to end the day there and go to bed. And, here I am, writing in my diary.
I'll write again soon.
Mitzy.

Ryan (10)
Hatchell Wood Primary Academy, Bessacarr

Doggy Day Out

Dear Diary,

This morning, I woke up and strode straight to Mum's room. I jumped right on her, asking for food. She got up, looking tired, and fed me some of my most favourite dog biscuits ever! Then I went outside and looked for the perfect place to do my business. The perfect spot, I spotted it right under Dad's apple tree that he'd been growing for ages. I ran around in circles until I found the right place. After that, I ran inside, too energetic. I wanted a walk - a big walk. I walked up to Dad and gave him the cute eyes look, so he had to say yes. It worked every time! Dad had his delicious breakfast, well, it looked like it! I thought to myself, *I wonder how yummy it is*, so I scratched on the side of the table to see if he would give me some. It didn't work. Mardily, Dad unhooked my lead off the hook while there I was, jumping in joy. I was so excited for this walk because I overheard Mum telling Dad to take me to the seaside. So, we got in the giant car. Obviously, I went in the front seat.

When we got there, I ran straight to the sea, running up and down. I went for a little swim. The water was just fine. After the swim, I ran up to Dad and shook my whole, furry mane all over him.

Oops, he didn't look happy. We went back home and I went straight to bed for a nap.
I had the most wonderful day. I'll write again soon.

Amelia Mccormack (10)
Hatchell Wood Primary Academy, Bessacarr

Pup Dup Jup

Dear Diary,

Today was awesome, fantastic, phenomenal! I woke up on my owner's bed, licked their face and in excitement rolled over on them. For some reason, they were in pain! Then I ran, slipping over every now and again, to the food cupboard and constantly scratched at the door. It annoyed Mum, but I'm a dog. I'll do anything for food!

When she got to open the door, it was a little too late! I kind of made a fun puddle by drooling for half a minute, oops!

It was hilarious watching Mum clean up. It took her ten minutes and by that time, I figured out how to get in: just do puppy eyes at Dad. Then he took me out for a walk instead of Mum and we did some quite odd things.

First, he threw a treat up at the tree - I'm not a cat. Then he threw a treat far away - I am *lazy!* Then he took off my lead so I ran away and looked for my house!

Trying to find my way home, I scavenged around, sniffing every piece of grass. But in front of me was a muddy path which looked sparkly because of my mind, so I followed it but could hear howls all around me.

In fear, I panted over to a small cave but that's where the wolves were! Before I got chance to run away, they surrounded me. Just then, I remembered puppy eyes! Once I finished my adorable encouragement device, I just walked away and renamed it to... my superpower!

Devon Farthing (10)
Hatchell Wood Primary Academy, Bessacarr

The Worst And The Best Day Of My Life

Dear Diary,
Let me introduce myself. I am ten years old. I was born December 5th, 2008 and I normally always play football and play on my Xbox. I am an expert in cars and my favourite car is a Lamborghini Aventador SVJ Roadster.
I woke up so early and brushed my teeth, washed my face and went downstairs. I was really hungry! My mum took me out for breakfast to a place called Yates'. I had a really tasty burger and chips. After my breakfast, we went shopping. We got home, we only got a couple of things. When I went upstairs, I went on my Xbox and after that, I had my tea. We had shepherd's pie. Then I went outside and played football, but the ball got kicked across the road by my brother and we couldn't get it back so I went inside and went on my Xbox. My mum said, "No!" so I just went to bed.

Thursday 23rd March, 2018
Dear Diary,
Today I went to a huge theme park called Flamingo Land - it was the best day of my life! I went on fast rides, they were so fast. I thought they were going a hundred miles per hour!

The day went really fast. It was home time. We got home for 9:30pm. I went straight to bed, it was the best day of my life!

Yuvraj (10)
Hatchell Wood Primary Academy, Bessacarr

Doggy Diary

Dear Diary,

Today was wooftastic! I woke up freezing, so I decided to let my owner know to turn the machine on. It usually warms me up. My owner calls it the heater. After a while, I eventually began to get too warm, so I scratched the back door so my owner would let me out but she never came so I barked! *Woof, woof! Scratch, scratch!* Finally, she came. After all that, I thought, *I need to do my business.* She opened the door and I sprang out. I felt really energetic.

Then, I saw a... squirrel! My worst enemy had come to taunt me again so, of course, I ran after it as fast as my German shepherd legs could carry me! But, once again, it escaped!

Suddenly, I could smell the sweet smell of treats coming from the patch of grass near the garage. I raced to it and started digging. It hurt my paws a little bit but I was so excited I couldn't stop! Finally, I found it. It wasn't as interesting as I'd thought but it would have to do after all that hard work digging. It has come in useful through as I'm writing in it now, lying on the sofa.

PS I'm not allowed to be lying on it but I should be allowed, shouldn't I? Write again soon.
Buddy.

Freya Rose Webster (10)
Hatchell Wood Primary Academy, Bessacarr

Doggy Diary: By Peggy

27th June, 2016.
Dear Diary,
I woke up to the sound of Alys' alarm going off. *Is it really half-past seven already?* I thought. I did my daily stretch and roll, got up and gave Bertie (my husband dog) a little kiss on the cheek. He was as miserable as ever!
I started scratching at Alys' door to tell her to get up and feed me. She gave me a choice of chicken or fish-flavoured biscuits. I chose chicken, my all-time favourite. As it was Sunday, I knew Alys had football and would take me out for a walk afterwards.
After football, her friend, Holly, came round and they took me and my hubby to the park. I once again got stuck in the same rabbit hole I always get stuck in. Alys came running to me and lifted me out. *Phew!*
Then, it came to my favourite part of the entire week: treat time! I wondered what she would give me. Pedigree Jumbo Sticks with extra chicken! I ran into William's room and found Bertie fast asleep. I jumped onto William's bed and snuggled up to him. I fell asleep.

What an exciting day I've had. What an amazing day!
Peggy.

Alys Catherine Spencer (10)
Hatchell Wood Primary Academy, Bessacarr

Diary Of A Wimpy Dog

Wednesday 25th

Dear Diary,

This week was the worst week. I was woken up by my owner, then we went downstairs for breakfast. After we finished, my owner went to school, so I went to bed. I woke up to eat and a tragic thing happened. The school called and said that my owner had fallen and broken his leg!

Thursday 26th

Dear Diary,

After they got home, it was so different. The boy had sticks and a white thing on his leg. We went to sleep. I woke up to play, but I couldn't because I forgot that the boy had broken his leg, it was a tragic thing.

Friday 27th

Dear Diary,

When we woke up, we went to the hospital. I didn't know why we went, but then I figured it out. We went to check his leg out and I was happy because the doctor said that we could get it off on Wednesday 2nd May!

Wednesday 2nd May
Dear Diary,
When we went to the hospital, I was so excited. Finally, we got there and the doctor took it off, then we went to play, then we went home to eat and play and do more normal things. I can't wait to go on a walk with the boy!

Adam (10)
Hatchell Wood Primary Academy, Bessacarr

Is This A Dream?

Dear Diary,

I ran around on my paws as my new owners packed a big, roaring machine. They called it a campervan, but I didn't like the roaring beast. It had shiny ears and it looked like there was another dog, just like me, inside them.

Before I knew it, there were hundreds of small beasts with yellow signs on the back and big ears. I think they're called wing mirrors, but I like calling them ears. I had my head out of the window and my tongue out of my mouth and then Alex, my brother, tried biting me, so my owner put him in the back (the tummy) of the monster.

After being in a long queue, I stretched my legs as I saw the wonderful beach. After having a good old nap, I ran into the sea, shaking my fur as I started swimming. I ran out of the sea and made it to my owner, then I dug a hole in the sand. I covered my body, but not my mouth, and before I could say 'woof', I was asleep. The next thing I knew, I was sleeping on a windowsill with Alex, watching my owners pack a campervan. I hope the dream comes true! Write again soon!

Jayden Samuel Ross (9)
Hatchell Wood Primary Academy, Bessacarr

All About My Bad Day!

Dear Diary,

Today, I woke up in the stables, bored, but suddenly everything I saw was wrecked and I didn't know why! My tack was on the floor! A horse called Sleepwalker was caught on the security cameras. Must have been that silly fool again! Even my favourite snack was gone, Asda's juicy apples. My owner, Jess, came a little later.

Jess took my head collar, wherever it was, and put it on my head. She led me into the field and left me there like she was abandoning me. A scary monster jumped out at me (really, it was just a plastic bag). She came back with my tack and a juicy apple to feed me and ride me. She took me to the ring and mounted me. It felt like there was an elephant on my back and a heavy one too! Her friend, Joannah set jumps out for us. I was playing on my phone and didn't see what I was doing. I faceplanted the floor! I had a great trip.

Jess untacked me, took me to my stable and put me back. Anyway, I now have a great big bump on my forehead!

Write to you soon, goodbye for now!

Paige Lucas (10)
Hatchell Wood Primary Academy, Bessacarr

A Day In The Life Of A Dog!

Dear Diary,
Today was the best day of my life. It started with me waking up and having my delicious breakfast. After breakfast, I started barking at my owner, Alfie.
I was saying, "Walkies!"
Alfie knew what I was saying so we set off on our walk. I ran around crazy in the garden, excited to go through my favourite woods and fields. My owner, Alfie, said I have to stay on my lead until I get into woods.
I barked and said, "Boring!"
We crossed the road into the woods. I eyed up a pigeon and slowly crept up on it. Sadly, it got away.
We arrived at the field and out of nowhere, my best friend, Willow, was licking me everywhere. I was telling him to get off and eventually, he did. We found a massive, muddy puddle. We decided to go roll in it, it was amazing and we got soaking wet! Alfie wasn't very happy so we went home. He washed me down until I was as clean as a whistle. After that, I decided to go to bed and rest my little legs.

Reece (9)
Hatchell Wood Primary Academy, Bessacarr

My Devilish Big Sister

Dear Diary,

My devilish big sister, called Charlotte, did something terrible to me. I'd just finished watching my favourite TV show, Blue Planet, when I followed my big brother upstairs. We brushed our teeth with each other and then we heard our sister coming up the stairs to have her teeth done.

I hate my big sister! I wanted to wind her up by getting her favourite dog cushion. I ran around my brother's room chasing after him with it. My sister screamed and got really angry at me for taking her cushion. She started chasing me around the landing and then pushed me down the stairs!

I hit my head on each step, getting bruises and cuts and then hit my head on the very bottom. I screamed and cried at the very bottom of the stairs and my sister was taken to her bedroom straight away. I heard her crying and that filled me with joy.

I'm struggling to write, I hope my agony doesn't happen again. I will get my revenge one day.

Joshua Wilkin (10)
Hatchell Wood Primary Academy, Bessacarr

The Best Day Of My Life

Dear Diary,
Today was a very surprising day. Now I have an owner! It all started at 8:40 in the morning when the shop opened and I was still eating my breakfast of kale. Straight away, the first person I spotted was a young boy about six or seven years of age. His hair was crazy! He ran over to me like he knew I was the one. He looked very excited. It was a warm day! He went to his parents and said, "Can I have a guinea pig?" I thought that this was my chance. I tried to get my friend as well because he asked for two. We played around, trying to look cute, rolling around, trying to be silly. For once in my life, I could be waking up in a beautiful little house! Then he said, "Look at this one!" Did he just say me? Silly old me? I jumped up into my soon-to-be-owner. I had been there for a year at that point, a very lonely year. So, that was my action-packed day!
I will write tomorrow about my first day of having an owner!

Lars (9)
Hatchell Wood Primary Academy, Bessacarr

Buttons

Dear Diary,

So, today, I left Amy (the person who bred my mum and dad) to go to a happy home and, get this, I am only two months old! When Amy picked me up, I started getting nervous because I knew where I was going. The family knocked on the door and Amy opened it. I saw my new owners, Sarah, Emma and Amy (a different Amy!) and their mum and dad! Amy gave me to Emma and she hugged me tightly. She put me into this box to go home. On the ride home, Sarah was taking pictures of me and stroking my white fur. When we finally arrived home, we went straight to the living room. Emma's dad got me out of the box and gave me to Sarah! She sat down and put me on her legs. I ran straight off them because her legs were on the floor! I went to her mum and she stroked me. She also fed me. Then I got put in my cage to rest and I was so afraid to go up the ramp. Anyway, I've got to go to sleep!
Toodles!

Sarah (10)
Hatchell Wood Primary Academy, Bessacarr

Doggy Days

Dear Diary,

Today, I woke up, jumping up and down on my owner, excited for the day. She fed me some dog food, it was delicious. Then, I accidentally did a poo on the floor. She wasn't going to be happy about that... I was so happy because we're getting a dog next week! My new brother. He's a Husky. We're going to be the bestest friends ever!

After that, my owner and I went for a nice walk with the sun blinding us. On our way back, I noticed my friend opposite us and I wanted to say hi. Straight after we got home, I collapsed on the floor, out of breath. Luckily, my owner, Jenna, once again fed me Pedigree dog food. She's the best. Somehow, Jenna bought dog toys before we came home and surprised me with them.

I'm really excited to get a brother. This is my last week without a buddy to live life with!

I'll write again soon.

Simon.

Szofia Buhajcsuk (10)

Hatchell Wood Primary Academy, Bessacarr

Kitty Days

Dear Diary,

Today was paw-tastic! Here is how it went.

I woke up my owner by meowing for food. She started mumbling, "In a minute!"

An hour of painful waiting later, she finally woke up. My owner climbed out of bed and ran downstairs. Yum! My favourite - chicken and salmon! I quickly ate so she could open the door and my adventure began. She opened the back door and went to slump on the couch. I ran outside as fast as I could. I went to next door's garden to catch some rabbits but I failed so I went to the pond and tried to catch some fish - yes! I caught a toad!

When I got home, Mother was terrified! She started screaming! My sister started petting me and saying, "Good girl!"

I got kind of scared and ran upstairs.

A couple of hours later, it was bedtime. I snuggled up with my owner and fell asleep. Write to you soon!

Katie Lynne Hoyle (10)
Hatchell Wood Primary Academy, Bessacarr

Dog Adventures

Dear Diary,

Today, I had a very dangerous day because my owner, Timmy, said not to go for a wander, but I did. I met up with Max and Jeff. We saw something unusual, we went into the woods and we all fell down a hole in the ground. Then, I saw a door, it looked very suspicious. Me, Max and Jeff all went in.

All three of us went running in to see if anyone was behind us, but there was no one there! "Wait a minute, what's that noise?" Jeff said.

There was only a forest, but it was a magical forest that had lots of trees and a massive house. It was a haunted house, the floorboards were creaking, the wind was howling. There were people there. We needed to go. "They're chasing me!" Max said. "Hide in a bush!"

Finally, I got back to my owner and gave me my favourite dinner: beef-flavoured Baker's Choice!

Rio (10)
Hatchell Wood Primary Academy, Bessacarr

Pet Shop With Buddy

10th January, 2019

Dear Diary,

Today was a paw-tastic day because, this morning, me and my owner were in a car. I hated the car, so I kept crying. As I did, my owner gave me a gentle rub which felt good.

When we arrived, my owner got me out of the car and I was terrified because I saw another big hairball on four legs (a dog)! But, it wasn't just me who saw it, my owner did too. She picked me up, I was better this way.

When we went through the huge doors, people were staring at me, so I barked and barked. While I was doing this, my mum was pulling me away from the people in the shop. All I could hear was people saying, "Look at that dog!"

Wagging my tail, my mum was picking up my favourite treats: chicken-flavoured bone bits! After that, we went home to see my sister, April.

I'll write again soon.

Buddy.

Ebony Angel Tucker (10)
Hatchell Wood Primary Academy, Bessacarr

Mr Butlings

Dear Diary,
Today was the best day ever! I got a new owner and a new home. I had to get rid of my old life at the fair, waiting for people to win me. But now, my life has changed quite a bit!
It all started at the fair when I was waiting for children to have a go at my game and win me as a prize. I felt like today was the day I'd get a new home. Suddenly, a little girl named Marie came to have a try on hook a duck (my game). She had a timer of one minute and caught one duck (number nine). Her prize was a choice between me and a doll. Of course she chose me! I'm the better looking one! She's named me Mr Butlings. I'm feeling so happy that I've got a new home and a new owner. Write again soon.
Mr Butlings.

Marie Walton (9)
Hatchell Wood Primary Academy, Bessacarr

A Day For An Adventure

Dear Diary,

On Saturday, I went for a walk in the park. I was excited because I love walks! My owner let me off my lead. I ran around the park, then I went to this tree. I found a little hole so I made it dog size - my size! I went down the hole and I found a trapdoor thing. Then I fell down and down, it was like going on forever! Then I hit the sweet ground with a thump! I was somewhere I'd never seen before. Then a cage fell on me. Then this man came to me and let me out of the cage. I felt nervous! Everybody loved me there. It was good there but I wanted to go home.

I went up this ladder and I was in a different land that made me laugh, but still, I wanted to go home! I went up and up and I finally found the park and my owner, then we went home.

Write to you soon.

Pearl.

Sarena Collin (10)
Hatchell Wood Primary Academy, Bessacarr

The Incredible Diary Of...

Wednesday 10th January
Dear Diary,
Today was the worst day at school. At break, I broke my arm. Someone tripped me up and I landed on my arm. I was in so much agony from the gall, I had to wear a sling until my mum came and picked me up from school. Then, we went to the hospital. The doctor didn't come until six hours later, then they said it would take a couple of hours for the cast to go on. Then they said it would take six months for the cast to come off and it would be healed after six months.

Tuesday 10th July
Dear Diary,
It's six months later! Today, I was feeling great and extraordinary. The cast was ready to come off. We all woke up and went to the hospital, the doctor came right away. She took the cast off and now, I can play video games again!

Jack (10)
Hatchell Wood Primary Academy, Bessacarr

The Incredible Diary Of...

Dear Diary,

It's me Batman, I have been feeling down, the powers of Marvel have been getting me down recently but me and Green Lantern have been working out how to beat Marvel. The plan is to get all the Justice League together (Wonder Woman, Superman, Aquaman, Cyborg and the Flash). We will meet in New York City and lure them into a trap on the Empire State Building.

When they walk in, I will be there and I will throw a smoke bomb so no one else can see them and then ambush them. I'm feeling super nervous because Thor might use his hammer. It's been a good day planning, now I'm going to have a Chimichanga with Green Lantern.

See you soon after the DC vs Marvel fight.
Batman aka Ashton.

Ashton Griffin
Hatchell Wood Primary Academy, Bessacarr

A Day In The Life Of Avah And Benji

Dear Diary,
Today was the best day ever because I got a new dog called Benji, he is a French Bulldog. He is seven months old. As soon as I got home, I gave Benji a choice of either a carrot or a chicken chew. He chose chicken. I put the chicken chew on the side and looked away for two minutes and he was jumping in a pool of drool. It was funny.
Later on, I took him on a walk. He chased after a squirrel. If I didn't catch him, the poor animal would be dead meat. We wandered into the woods and he jumped into a puddle. It was funny, but we had to go home.
As soon as we got home, I put him in the bath. By the end of bathtime, there was more water on the floor than in the tub!
See you soon.

Avah Grace Evans (10)
Hatchell Wood Primary Academy, Bessacarr

Dean's Diary

Dear Diary,

I had a fantastic day because I went to the fair and it was fun! I went on the waltzers and the Ferris wheel and the flip flop. It was good fun because the fair was really big! I found some gold and I was really excited...

I was really excited to spend it, it was so expensive. It was not just gold, there was a whole entire treasure chest. It was exciting for me because I was really happy. The gold was kept in a safe place.

Dear Diary,

Today I bought a mansion, a yellow Lamborghini and so many other cars. I bought a house for my friends, it was big! I was feeling better already! I thought this day would not come in a million years. I was amazed that I'd found gold!

Joshua (10)
Hatchell Wood Primary Academy, Bessacarr

A Purr-Fect Day!

27th December, 2016
Dear Diary,
Today was an amazing day. I got a cat who is two years old. I've called her Meme and I love her very much! We went to Pets At Home and I loved a dog called Catchy but when I saw Meme, I loved her more.

Later on today at 8pm, I gave Meme her fish-flavoured cat food. I had a little sniff myself but it smelt like rotten eggs, ew! Mum and Dad watched me feed her and I saw happiness spread across their faces.

When it was bedtime, I kissed my parents on the cheek and ran upstairs with Meme to write this in my diary. I have loved today. I wonder if tomorrow will be even better. Goodbye for now.
Melissa.

Melissa Malam (10)
Hatchell Wood Primary Academy, Bessacarr

Me When I Get Old As A Dog!

Dear Diary,

Yesterday was rough, I got no sleep so in the morning I felt weird, and so I went to the toilet and, you know what happened. Anyway, my owner, Fred, took me on a walk and there stood another dog! It was a golden retriever! I was very jealous and I barked and barked until they finally walked away down the path. Then, at that very moment, a monkey swung by the trees as I did my business on the so-called 'toilet' on the ground. We weren't in the Amazon Jungle! Very, very peculiar!

When we got home, my owner, Fred, gave me a Baker's Choice dog treat. I must say, it's my favourite kind of food!

From Bonesy.

Cruz Walter Dodds (9)
Hatchell Wood Primary Academy, Bessacarr

My Dog Rio

Saturday

Dear Diary,

Today I went on an exciting walk with my dog, Rio. We went through the woods and over the stream. It was good to go on that amazing walk with my dog.

After the walk, we went home to relax on the sofa and Rio went to bed so he could rest and get his energy back for his other walk on Sunday.

Sunday

Dear Diary,

When me and Rio came back from the walk on Saturday, we were very exhausted so we both went to bed.

The next morning was a boring, rainy day so me and Rio just sat in the house all day until it was summer again.

Hayden Snodin (10)
Hatchell Wood Primary Academy, Bessacarr

The Incredible Diary Of...

Dear Diary,

As I was tranquilly and peacefully waking up, I heard shouting.

"Help! Wakanda is coming to an end!"

I frantically shook, wondering what the nonsense was about. Then I found the problem... The barrier was getting attacked! I said, "It's impossible! How can this be?"

As soon as I said that, eerie spine-chilling lightning attacked as rain was pouring down. An omen, I reckoned. *Beep!* There was one hour and thirty minutes to get the mind-blowing machines that could get rid of the foolish people or even monsters attacking the barrier.

"Yes!" I said, and started dancing and singing. "Ha, you're never going to get me!" I did it again and jinxed it. Now there was only one hour till the barrier was going down! I strictly insisted, "Get my armour, these brats are going to hospital! Put the barrier down! Wakanda forever!"

As I was bravely going to attack, my army scampered into the distance, leaving me alone to fight...

Saif Ally (9)
Hatfield Academy, Sheffield

Charlie And The Diary Entry

Tuesday 25th March, 2019
Dear Diary,
Today was the scariest (but coolest and happiest) day of my life! It was scary because it was super nerve-racking.
I was walking home under the bright, dazzling stars. I looked like a living skeleton because my poor non-wealthy family had no money. This was because my father's business shut down, so everyone got fired. I froze. I gasped for air... I found one pound in a little dip that was in the road! My eyes and tastebuds watered with excitement. I ran faster than the world's fastest car. I barged into a line and I finally was served.
"One Fudgemallow, please."
I bought one. I shook with fear and I was shaking harder than a running engine. I opened it...
My body nearly shut down in shock. I screamed, "I got the last golden ticket!"
I ran home but got stopped by the police. They thought I'd shoplifted, but the cashier backed me up and said I didn't.
I carried on running, crowds of people chasing me with sorrow in their eyes because they couldn't get the ticket for their child. As quick as a flash, I turned into an alleyway and I escaped everybody.

"We're going to be millionaires in chocolate!" I mumbled when I got home.

Wednesday 26th March, 2019
Dear Diary,
I told everybody what happened.
"You what?"
"I have a golden ticket and I've decided Grandpa Joe's coming!"
I shook with excitement. I realised they didn't listen, but Grandpa Joe did. We're both going to the chocolate factory tomorrow!

Oliver Sampson (8)
Hatfield Academy, Sheffield

The Incredible Diary Of...

20th September

Dear Diary,

Today was the best but scariest day ever! So today I was making my stringy incredible web and this little boy tried to put me in a glass and kill me but my very good, amazing friend, Fern, saved me. Do you wanna know how she saved me? Well, this young boy was Fern's brother so she took the glass out of his hand and let me free.

So, later on, I started to build my web because I was starting to get a little hungry. Soon after, I had my dinner and talked to Wilbur. I told him about how Fern saved my life. Anyway, Wilbur asked me if I would go to the fair with him. I said yes. This fair thing is about if Wilbur will win the big grand prize! (Of course he will!)

4th November

Dear Diary,

We finally arrived at the fair. It looked amazing! Do you want to know what was there? There was a candyfloss machine, a hot dog place, shining lights and of course Wilbur's barn! The barn was so big for just a petite piglet (now grown to a pig).

I carefully climbed out of the cart and waddled to the barn. Ouch! My heart skipped two beats! I woke up and didn't feel very good. Straight away I knew... I was pregnant! Oh no! What should I do? Okay, it's fine! I was just a little dramatic!
I can't wait for my spiderlings to arrive and to meet my good friend Wilbur. I do hope they like him as much as I do. Anyway, I've gotta go and do some spider stuff. You know I like catching flies and spinning webs. Bye!

Ruby Jean Broomhead (9)
Hatfield Academy, Sheffield

The Incredible Diary Of...

Saturday 22nd January, 2019
Dear Diary,
I was walking by when I saw rotten cheese. Slowly, I was about to touch the cheese when I was stopped by Greg. Greg said, "Once there was a boy who touched the cheese and he got the rotten cheese touch. The only way to get rid of it was to touch someone else. So he touched a girl. The girl touched someone and it was a disaster. Friend turning on friend. Teachers turning on teachers. People turning on people. Then suddenly, it stopped when a man washed his hands..."

Sunday 23rd January, 2019
Dear Diary,
A boring, ordinary day.

Monday 24th January, 2019
Dear Diary,
I decided to pull a prank on Miss Tourzani, so I went and got some salt and apple juice. Slowly pouring some salt in the apple juice, I ensured that the coast was clear. I stirred carefully. I heard a teacher walking by. I stirred quicker and gave it to Miss Tourzani. I smirked. She drank it and started coughing...

Tuesday 25th January, 2019
Dear Diary,
I heard Miss Tourzani has a phobia of spiders. I bought some robot-controlled spiders. At 4am, I put lots of spiders everywhere. I kept the tarantula. When everyone went to school, I controlled the spider and it went on Miss Tourzani's head. She screamed so loud, all the birds on top of the school roof flapped hastily away. Saif laughed so loud even Australia could hear it!

Al-Sadig Bakhit (9)
Hatfield Academy, Sheffield

The Incredible Diary Of...

Dear Diary,
If I had to describe how I am feeling right now, then I am feeling like a piece of poop! Ugh, my overprotective, ignorant, annoying dad completely humiliated me in front of the *whole* village! Underneath the glimmering, glistening sun, I slowly sneaked past my stupid, (I hope he doesn't see this) idiotic dad talking to the village council and hastily ran to my kind, loving grandma dancing on the ocean shore.

As sneaky as a ninja, every night I secretly creep out of our cabin whilst my foolish, cruel dad is sleeping (not allowing him to nag me) and run to my grandma who is always beautifully dancing on the ocean. By the way, the reason why I hate my dad is because I love staring at the deep blue ocean and whenever I try to attempt to sail on a boat, my dad says, "No, Moana! You belong here!" and he keeps completely eliminating my dreams. My grandma is the only one who understands me. As always, I sneaked to my grandma tonight. I went to dance with the sea with her.

"The sea... chose you!" my grandma muttered. Suddenly, I saw a small wave of the ocean appeared above my head.

Uh-oh, flashback time! I could remember that exact same thing happening to me when I was a baby, but can it be? Now I'm getting a little woozy so I think I'll stop writing now...
Moana.

Sarah Ahmed Maisari (9)
Hatfield Academy, Sheffield

The Incredible Diary Of...

Dear Diary,
Today has been the most action-packed day ever! This day was the best.
So I woke up this morning only to find Phoebe and Jay (my owners) to be gone from upstairs! I just wanted a morning stroke from them! I wondered to myself out loud that the ring I'd heard this morning was what had made them wake up at 6:30am.
Suddenly, I heard the front door open. They really were gone. Then I realised I could explore their rooms!
So I went into Jay's room and found his bed all messy. However, I still lay on it. I lay there for about one sleepless uncomfortable hour trying to go to sleep. I got off the bed and explored his wardrobe (he never closes it). I found a giant bucket of toys. He also has another shelf so I climbed up there. Yep, more clothes. Boring! I thought, *let's go to Phoebe's room!*
In Phoebe's room, as quick as a cheetah, I spotted something fluffy. OMG! I ran faster than the speed of light and pounced onto the bed. Then I fell asleep for two hours.

I then looked in Phoebe's drawers for something to play with. The first easy-opening drawer I opened had clothes. Boring! I opened the next drawer and I found my favourite toy! I played with it for three hours. Then I heard a noise. Phoebe and Jay were back. So that was my day,
Pepsi.

Phoebe Crookes (9)
Hatfield Academy, Sheffield

Rapunzel's Escape
An extract

Dear Diary,
Today has been the best day of my life ever! You will never guess what happened to me.
So, it all started when I woke up in my tall castle and glared out of the window. I had this strange feeling that I wanted to escape. I had been living in that tall castle for years and had never thought of going outside. (I'd probably been living in that dump for my whole life!) Surprisingly, I'd never run out of food. I thought I couldn't get out, it was just so tall.
I was thinking, *I don't have a long, strong and sturdy rope so... I could use my hair! OMG! Why didn't I think of this before? I have never been outside the castle and the world might be scary... But I must not think negatively, I must escape!*
Excitedly, I ran for a large picnic blanket, an even bigger basket, food, clothes, cups, a kettle, plates, toiletries and much more. Then I said, "Urm, bye!"
I tied my hair to a round hook on the window ledge and off I went! It felt like a roller-coaster ride and I whizzed as fast as... a girl on long hair!

As soon as I reached the bottom, I screamed. There was a strong, green, spiky thing. Then I began to walk. It looked strange when I was actually on the ground. The trees were tall and vast and I began to explore...

Leila Zeb (9)
Hatfield Academy, Sheffield

The Incredible Diary Of...

Dear Diary,
Today I will be writing about Vikings because we are learning about Vikings travelling to Norway, Sweden and Denmark. They would get tired of travelling to those places. They had battles in Norway, Sweden and Denmark. There were Anglo Saxons vs the Vikings. The Vikings had shields and sword hammers. They went to a battle in June 1618.

Some Vikings died and Anglo Saxons all died too. When dying, they actually didn't die, pranked ya! The Vikings went in their little houses and drank tea. They went to another battle to fight the Anglo Saxons. Vikings won the battle.

They got tired of going to battle. They went to sleep and heard a noise. It was the Anglo Saxons. They said, "We can kill more Anglo Saxons! We are not going to die, don't worry. We will kill them! Attack!"

They fought for fifteen minutes. The winner was the Vikings. I told you they would win. They won new swords.

They went back to sleep and the Vikings then travelled to Sweden, Norway and Denmark again. They went to Norway where there were a lot of other Vikings.

Then they went to Iceland to buy food because they didn't have any more food.
The Vikings then went to Roman Britain to find horses, ready for their final battle with the Anglo Saxons.

Amelia Isobell Lucas (9)
Hatfield Academy, Sheffield

The Mermaid Spell!

Dear Diary,

I have had the worst year of my life! I was in a boat, trying to fix it, but someone took the rope off it and I could not figure out how to work it. I was scared until a new girl from school came and put this thing in the engine, which was just what I needed, and then I told her I could not work the boat. I then heard the engine go on and then we were moving on the water and my friend, Donut, did a jump on the boat while my other friend, Pringle, was staring at it.

The engine ran out of fuel and we needed to paddle to where the nearest layby was. We were in a hole that was at the end of a cave and we had to swim out of it.

The next day, my friends and I had a show. I had a bath and suddenly got a long tail and looked... well, I turned into a mermaid! I went to Donut's house and told her everything. After I told her, she said it happened to her and Pringle said it happened to her as well! We all were really freaked out.

"Maybe we should go back there once again?"

"No, we cannot do that!"
"Let's tell our parents."
"No, we cannot do anything or say anything to anyone at all..."

Brooke Stringer (9)
Hatfield Academy, Sheffield

The Incredible Diary Of The Game

Dear Diary,

Today was an *epic* day! My team played FC Barcelona and won! Well, have I ever lost anyway? First, I had to change into my comfortable away kit and get my beautiful boots ready.

Yesterday I arrived in Barcelona. I stepped out of my luxurious limo and went inside my five-star hotel. Then I jumped on my bed! I was actually surprisingly nervous. Then it was match day. I slowly walked over to the fridge and got a nice yoghurt with a raspberry in it. After I ate it, I quickly took a shower and jumped into my football kit and got into my limo.

Fifteen minutes later, I arrived at the stadium. I then came into the stadium and put my football boots on in the locker room.

Moments later, I came out onto the pitch! We shook hands and then got into position. Then we went on with the game.

It was into their box but they cleared it! The defender put it to me and then I passed to the other winger. They passed back to me and I hit the ball as hard as I could towards the net. *It was a goal!*

I was as happy as a child on Christmas day. All the fans were too!
Tyler Memmott (9)
Hatfield Academy, Sheffield

The Incredible Diary Of...

Dear Diary,

Today was the weirdest and most puzzling day ever! So I was in my warm, cosy bed and my alarm went off. *Beep beep!* I realised it was Friday so I woke up with my unicorn teddy and walked to the chocolate shop.

"One sprinkle surprise please!"

I let it spread across my tongue lovingly. When I went outside there was a puzzling, petrifying portal and a sign saying A Series of Unfortunate Events. I tried to dodge it but it sucked me in! My heart was pounding. Spirals swirled through my head. When I could see again I saw devils and fire raising! I felt petrified. I looked around and an imp said, "If you want to stay and not get killed, you have to pass a riddle."

I said okay. I was puzzled.

"What flies with a pitchfork that rhymes?"

"A devil?"

"Correct, you may stay."

"Honey, it's pancake day!"

Then I realised it was a *dream!* I was back to my normal, cute life again.

George Lyall (9)
Hatfield Academy, Sheffield

The Incredible Diary Of...

Thursday 22nd January, 2015
Dear Diary,
Today has been the most frightening day ever here in Antarctica. So it all happened when I (a baby penguin) was playing with my friend outside until we heard something crack. I tried not to move one bit... but it cracked even more and then... I went floating away. I yelled for my mother but she couldn't hear me. I was miserable! I didn't know what to do. I panicked. My heart was beating fast. So I just decided to go to sleep and figure this out in the morning.

Friday 23rd January, 2019
Dear Diary,
It was morning and I seemed happy but sad at the same time. As quick as a flash, I realised that I was on sand earlier. I'm not used to this or the kind of weather it is. But that isn't the problem. I need to get home. I hope that somebody will find me and that my friends will have told my mum what happened.
I'm wondering what to do, I can hear somebody calling my name...!

Sharifah Wright (9)
Hatfield Academy, Sheffield

The Incredible Diary Of...

Dear Diary,

Today has been the best day! Firstly, I was quietly strolling through the scary, mysterious forest when suddenly, I heard a tiger! Then I began to run, my heart was as fast as a rocket. The tiger was getting closer to me!

I turned back and there was dust everywhere! Then the tiger jumped over my head, it started attacking the other tigers. I kept running, I was terrified.

I eventually stopped running and the tiger came closer to me as it stared at me. It didn't do anything to me, I didn't know if the other tigers were going to do the same thing.

I wondered if the tiger wanted to be my friend or was it trying to trick me into doing what it wanted me to do? I decided that I wanted it to be my friend.

I noticed that it pointed to a moving bush, so I looked into the bush and it had baby tigers inside! Were these the tiger babies? The tiger did talk in tiger language and the tiger and I stayed there for a while.

James Fu (8)
Hatfield Academy, Sheffield

The Incredible Diary Of...

Dear Diary,

Today has been the most interesting but fun day of my life. It all started when I was peacefully sleeping under some trees and then I heard a noise... what could it be? Listening carefully, I heard somebody walking towards me! Under the trees, I rapidly scrambled to find a safe hiding place but I couldn't find one!

My mind was a blizzard with thoughts racing through my head. *Ping!* A thought struck my mind. Because I was a dragon, a Night Fury, I could fly to get away.

Soaring through the trees, I knew I wouldn't get attacked but then my black, scaly wing got torn by one of the branches. I needed my wings to fly but my wing was broken which meant that I was falling!

I knew this was bad news, the fact that my wing was broken and then the fact that I landed in front of the human! What would I do? I thought this would be the end of me...

Emma Isabella Pyecroft (9)
Hatfield Academy, Sheffield

Louis' Life

Dear Diary,

I've just chucked all of my maths books away. I do feel bad but then I mostly feel fine. So it's near Christmas, um, well it's the 1st of December, I've got nothing for my family or my girlfriend. Well right now I'm on Amazon.com. So I have £30.99p but what could I buy? My girlfriend is called Meg and she loves slime so I could buy her some slime.

Tuesday 2nd December

Dear Diary,

So I've bought my girlfriend some slime, it will come next week on Monday because it's being shipped all the way from New York. So I need to buy my mum, my dad and my brother a Christmas gift but what could I buy them with £29.00? So my brother really wants the Starlink battle for Atlas and he's already got the console so he needs another character, so I can buy him the Joe character. So I've bought my brother the Joe character so now I've got £28.00 so now I can buy my mum some perfume and my dad some aftershave and that will leave me with £19.00.

Monday 8th December
Dear Diary,
All of the things have come.

Christmas Day
Dear Diary,
My girlfriend and my family loved their gifts, I'm so proud of myself, I'm the best.

Lucy Johnson (7)
Serlby Park Academy, Bircotes

The Incredible Diary Of...

Dear Diary,

Lily here again. I have an annoying big brother called Lewis. He was ten years old yesterday. He is always off on an adventure but I never know where to.

It was Saturday morning and Mum was busy doing housework, I was so bored but I had an idea! I thought that this will be the day I find out what my brother gets up to.

I crept upstairs and went to my brother's bedroom door, I tried to look through the keyhole but I couldn't see a thing. I thought I would sit for a while to see if I could hear anything. I sat for five minutes, then all of a sudden I heard a thud, a loud bang and a whizzing noise. It made me jump so I suddenly jumped up and looked through the keyhole again, this time I saw that his bedroom was empty! And the bedroom window was open!

I ran downstairs in shock and ran into the front garden. To my horror my brother Lewis was dressed in a blue and red suit and he had a cap on back to front and he was flying!

Lewis saw me looking at him and he flew down. He dragged me to the back of the shed and made me promise not to tell anyone, not even Mum.

If I kept it a secret he promised he would take me flying one day!
Wow, that is a massive secret!

Esther Clarke (8)
Serlby Park Academy, Bircotes

The Situation

Saturday 10:48

Dear Diary,

Yesterday, the most tragic thing happened on our way to Spain. Me and my family were involved in a plane crash... At the minute, I can still barely breathe. Amongst the chaos, there were people everywhere.

Some were seriously injured, others died at the scene. Luckily for me, I'm still here (otherwise I wouldn't be writing this!) But unfortunately my... my family aren't!

I'm at the hospital having to have scans the same as everyone else. My family, as I said earlier, are in a ward altogether. Yesterday, my feelings changed in all the sad ways. It was so dramatic and shocking for me. Sorrow built up in me and happy memories came from their hiding spots. I'm so eager to be able to see everyone again.

Sunday 11:24

Dear Diary,

So we are all back home now but we need to stay here and rest. I have a bad pain in my stomach and I keep letting out big gasps. Apart from that, I'm pretty much fine! (Fortunately!)

Mary-Beth Stephenson (11)
Serlby Park Academy, Bircotes

The Football's Diary

Dear Diary,

Today I have had an amazing/crazy day, because I was put on a gigantic field with lots of boys who started to kick me around. All of a sudden, I was kicked so hard I went flying into the dark terrifying place called the forest.

Suddenly, I heard a hissing sound. It only took me a couple of seconds to realise that I was being deflated, for a thorn had got into me. I heard loud thumps. I got so worried they might hear the hissing. I tried to roll over to make the hissing a bit fainter but the thumps got louder and louder until they stopped...

I turned around and I saw.... a face. It was staring straight at me, it took me a few minutes to realise it was just a bird. Then I heard some more thumps but louder and they sounded more like a boy's feet. I was so relieved that when I sighed, the hissing got louder. The boy picked me up. When I got on the field he put some air in me and carried on kicking me.

Goodbye Diary.

From Football.

Sophia Sana (9)
St Oswald's Academy, Finningley

All About A Pencil

Dear Diary,

My name is Lilly, I live at school on a giant table in a pencil pot. Every morning I get written with. Every day the giant children use me too rough. I wonder who is going to use me today and what will I be writing about.

This morning I woke up in a shock. I was grabbed out of the pencil pot and was written with, I was writing out the nine times table in a maths book. They wrote with me so rough that a big accident happened, my lead broke.

Guess what happened next. I got squished in a blazer that you call a pencil sharpener. It was awful, pieces of wood were coming off of me. I felt like a pencil that was put inside a dog's mouth and got wet and chewed to pieces. I just hope that never happens.

A little girl asked if she could sit outside and draw. So she rapidly ran to the drawer with the paper in and she took me outside. When the bell rang she went in and left me outside. How dare she! I was cold.

Somehow a dog got into the school and put me in his soggy wet disgusting mouth. Oh no, this is what I didn't want to happen...

Just as I was picked up by him, he ran out of the school. I felt like I was in a pencil sharpener getting pieces of wood chopped off. He took me home and I was actually enjoying myself sunbathing in a fluffy dog bed. Luckily the dog's owner had a little girl who went to the same place that I came from, so when the adult went to school to pick her little girl up, she brought the dog for a walk. The dog suddenly dropped me on the floor at the school. The teacher saw one of her pencils on the floor so she took me back inside my pencil pot. I was exhausted after my day.

Darcie Mae Whitaker (8)
St Oswald's Academy, Finningley

A Turtle

Dear Diary,
I am a turtle and my name is Sheldon. My day has been a day like no other. I was having a swim in my favourite coral reef when all of a sudden, I heard the shrieks of a thousand fish in terror coming my way. "Run!" screamed many fish and before I could look up, a net made of strong rope had trapped me. I was trapped for hours and hours and hoped for someone with great strength to save me. I was isolated and sad.

Before long, I could see movements in the dark gloomy distance. There were three unknown figures swimming to me. These strange figures didn't look like friends, they looked worse. I only just noticed who these figures were, but it was too late to call for help. The figures were hammerhead sharks that looked like they hadn't eaten in three days. I could tell they were after me. They asked if I wouldn't mind if I could be their first meal in a while. "No," I replied.

"Well, you're going to have to," one shark said with an evil grin. The sharks got closer and closer.

In the blink of an eye, a whale the size of a towering skyscraper dashed at the three sharks. "Go away and never come back," yelled the whale.

"Okay," replied the horrified sharks, swimming away as fast as they could. "Are you okay?" asked the friendly whale.
"Yes, and please could you help me out?" I asked.
"Yes I can," he replied. Then I got out and came home and invited the whale.

Gregor Scott (9)
St Oswald's Academy, Finningley

The Amazing Game Of Liverpool Vs Everton

Dear Diary,

A few days ago I went to a massive game against Everton. Suddenly the whistle blew, the humongous crowd was shouting out, "Get a goal." I was very nervous. I passed to my friend Mane, I passed the ball to him because I was scared I would do something wrong.

In a blink of an eye, an Everton player tackled Mane. He ran down the pitch and scored a goal. It was 1-0 to Everton. It was a disaster for Liverpool. Quickly the ball was passed to me, I ran down the field so fast nobody could see me, all of a sudden I kicked the ball so fast it went into the net. All the crowd was shouting, "Take that Everton." I was so happy I scored a goal, it was 1-1.

It was half-time, everyone went to get a beer at the bar or get a pie from Pukka Pie. While everyone was getting drinks, we were training for the second half.

When everyone got back, the game started. We went to the bottom of the pitch like we had fire in us and Mane scored an amazing goal. Everyone was cheering, but the whistle went, the goal wasn't counted. "Boooo... booooo!" shouted the crowd.

Minutes passed, the game was nearly over. I got passed to, but someone kicked the ball away from me, it was a penalty. There were two minutes left, I kicked the ball, it went in the goal! Everyone was happy we won.

Harris Chapman (8)
St Oswald's Academy, Finningley

The Diary Of A Tortoise

Dear Diary,

Today I was so excited. I went to tortoise school and we got told we were going on a trip from England to Greece! We got our things together and got on an aeroplane. I was strapped in safely, but everyone else was running (walking) about. One of them was in the cockpit.

When we got to Greece, we went into a tiny tortoise hotel. I shared a room with my friend, Harry. We were in the Hermann's suite because we were both Hermann's tortoises.

The next day, we were told to pack up to go to Crete. We were going there on a boat. I packed up my little suitcase and hopped on. The journey took a few hours, so by the time we got there we went to our rooms.

The morning after, we had dandelions for breakfast. After breakfast, I felt upset because I missed my owner.

Later on, we met people who we were going to be pen pals with. My pen pal was called Shelly. That day we got to go on a journey with them. Also, we got to meet each other's owners. Shelly stayed with me in England for a few days.

We are still penpals now and still write to each other.
Speedy the tortoise.

Joseph Baker (9)
St Oswald's Academy, Finningley

The Incredible Pencil

Dear Diary,
Today was awesome, I was just minding my own business when I saw a weird metal thing. I thought *I'm a pencil, nobody will attack me*, so I went up to it. It was grey with metal bits inside. I thought it was just a toy so I went away. I felt sad as I was being bullied.
But today was unusual, instead of being made a fool of, people stood open-mouthed at me, then I saw why. I felt petrified. It wasn't a toy, it was a sharpener!
I ran or should I say hopped, to the next table. The sharpener was just like me, alive. The sharpener was way faster than me so I rampaged through the room.
Then I was shoved into the sharpener, but when I came out I was beautiful. My point was there as bold as a piece of black paper. The process was painful, I mean being sharpened, oww. But soon after admiring my amazing point, everybody was applauding.
Then I thought hard, who had sharpened me? Nobody knew except Pen. Pen was the only pen in the class so I went over to Pen and said proudly,

"Who has put my amazing point on?"
"I did!" And then we became BFFs.

Kathryn Rose Beasley (9)
St Oswald's Academy, Finningley

The Diary Of Hermione Granger

Dear Diary,
After the school holidays I went to a place called Hogwarts, it was a witch and wizardry school. I couldn't go in a car there, I had to go on a train, but not a normal train, it was on a witch and wizard train. It was called Hogwarts Express! There were sweets on the train like pumpkin pasties, chocolate frogs and Bertie Botts' Every Flavoured Bean. There is bogey-flavoured, vomit-flavoured and more.
When I arrived at Hogwarts, Professor Dumbledore gave the whole of Hogwarts an assembly.
Then everyone started talking about the chamber of secrets, so I thought to myself, what is the chamber of secrets? Then I went to the library to look up the chamber of secrets.
It said the last time it opened a girl called Moaning Myrtle died and became a ghost. I thought I better ask Moaning Myrtle what happened, so I did. "Hi, do you remember anything about the chamber of secrets?"
She said, "No..."

Avilon Pawson (8)
St Oswald's Academy, Finningley

Purple Pen Day At School

Dear Diary,

I am a purple pen and my name is Lilla. I love relaxing in the pot. Me and my friend Yellow love going on journeys.

This morning, I woke up in my soft bed but to humans it is called a pot, however my family calls it our home.

Today, it is purple pen day at St Oswald's Academy. I love purple pen day because I get used a lot in one day. However, today I am feeling a little bit scared and worried because what if I get trodden on, or worse, snapped?

So, I set off on my journey around school, Yellow was with me. Yellow and I went to the tremendous Year 5 classroom. It was a mess! After that, me and Yellow ran to Year 3, we ran because it was in the other building!

Ten minutes later, we finally got to Year 6, it was messy as well. I thought that Year 6 was the messiest class in the whole school!

Last of all, I went back to Year 4 class, where I was before. It was an amazing day in school today!

Lilla Rose Ward (9)
St Oswald's Academy, Finningley

The Incredible Diary Of... Alioski

Dear Diary,
One beautiful day, I was playing a game of football for Leeds against Norwich in the league. I was a goal machine, passing the ball about and making a lot of runs with the ball. After that 4-0 win, I celebrated with my family telling them how good I was (bragging).

Two dark petrifying nights passed and then it was training having a good laugh, that soon went away and suddenly on that day I saw a new face in training. After training finished I walked over to him and yelled, "Who are you, you did well out there, me and Pablo will work with you."

A couple of days later, we had a game and the new man Kemar Roofe was in the starting line up. However, the boy was a monster.

In that very game, Roofe scored two goals and I scored one, something had changed.

As games went on he kept on scoring and I did not score any goals at all. I learned not to brag and I also learned to work as a team.

Oliver Storey (9)
St Oswald's Academy, Finningley

The Journey Of Pac-Man

Dear Diary,

Today has been crazy. I was going around the dark brick maze on level seventeen when the guy playing reached a high score of fifteen thousand! After all the dots I had eaten, I felt stuffed, in fact I was becoming bigger, I was getting larger.

Then, I noticed the screen getting cracked, I was getting too big for the game. The man playing ran away as shards of glass flew off the screen. I rolled across the floor smashing Paper Boy, Tetris and Space Invaders. Luckily I rolled into a gymnasium so I could lose some weight.

For some reason I got quite a lot of weird looks from people. I went on a treadmill, although I just rolled off. I lifted weights, I had to use my head because I didn't have arms.

After doing more exercise, (I mean challenging someone to a dance fight) I went back through the hole in the wall and one of the staff helped me back into my game. I had a very extraordinary day.

Geno Eagle (9)
St Oswald's Academy, Finningley

The Incredible Diary Of... Lionel Messi

Dear Diary,
Today was overwhelming. I went to the hectic World Cup with my amazing manager, Marcelo Bielsa. He is the epic manager of Leeds United. Today we were training for one joyful magic game. Just then, Marcelo Bielsa rapidly ran over to Dybala and Di Maria. "I want you to be just as good as Lionel Messi."

Dear Diary,
I was so ready for the match today I really wanted to get there faster. Five minutes later it was time to kick off. As quick as a flash the football got kicked, I was so scared. The ball came to me, it was near the net. I had a shot! Yeaaahhh I scored. The stadium went so loud. I went over to my team's fans and celebrated. Like the wind, Mbappe rapidly ran down the wing, he crossed it into the box, Griezmann scored. 1-1!
In the last few seconds, Di Maria passed to Dybala, Dybala ran up the wing, he crossed it in to me. I scored. Yeaaaaaah!

Alfie Harrison Taylor (9)
St Oswald's Academy, Finningley

Into Poopland

Dear Diary,

Wow, just wow. Yesterday a huge portal appeared in my unilluminated room. I slid out of my basket and dived in like a rugby player. In a flash I landed in brown, grubby sludge. Mousse! I lunged and my mouth chomped through chunk after chunk. I realised it was poo! Yuck! I leapt gracefully out, landing silently.

In an instant, a monstrous mountain grew, massive outcrops of the cliff face crumbling like sand. The once solid ground beneath me shook violently. I vaulted off the cliff face onto the mountain of sick before me. Then, all went black.

As I drowsily woke up, a radiant heat engulfed my bum suddenly. It wasn't a mountain, it was a volcano! The hot urine trickled down, the jagged cliff melting as the urine slid down towards me...

Harry Hermiston (8)
St Oswald's Academy, Finningley

The Incredible Diary Of... A Weird Guinea Pig

Dear Diary,

Today was both exciting and awful. I was just eating some delicious dandelions when I crunched something hard. I heard whirring sounds, I was getting bigger and bigger and bigger! Soon I was the size of my owner. I looked at my paws, I had fingers!

I walked across to the stairs. Walking was hard on two feet. I soon got the hang of it. I ate some bread thing. It was as disgusting as poop. I was scared, could I survive eating human food forever? Did Charlie miss me? Hopefully that's what friends do, right?

It was tea time, we had something called mansdudo. I ate some, it was quite nice actually. Then the whirring sound came again. I was shrinking. Soon I was in my cage again, relieved to see my friend. What a great day.

Eleanor Spencer (9)
St Oswald's Academy, Finningley

The Diary Of A Tiny Man Called Ant-Man

Dear Diary,

Today something crazy happened. I woke up and I was as big as an ant, or maybe smaller. I was so small I took ten minutes to get out of my towering bed. I got dressed after having a bath in the sink. I rode my dog and jumped on to the bin and onto the kitchen counter and opened the door.

I ran into someone's sandcastle. "It's caving in!" I said out loud. But I got out. After I got out I saw a shark somehow, it kept on diving to try and get me.

A lab picked me up called the robotic lab. Its hand brought me up into the lab. "Ant-Man it worked!"

"What worked?"

"The potion."

"Oh yeah." Now it's time to fight crime!

Joseph Duncan (9)
St Oswald's Academy, Finningley

Mario's Mystery

Dear Diary,
Today was overwhelming, I was just walking down the long, smooth road and I heard a mysterious noise! I wondered what it was. As quick as a flash I ran back to my house. It had disappeared! I said quietly, "Is anyone there?"
All I could hear now was laughing. Suddenly my house appeared! I walked slowly through the door. It was a cave! There were bats hanging moving in the wind. There was a mysterious figure in the background. I said, "Who are you?" He said, "I'm your brother...."

Alex Austin (9)
St Oswald's Academy, Finningley

The Journey Of Pac-Man

Dear Diary,

One day I was minding my own business when suddenly I got teleported. It looked like some kind of maze. Suddenly I started to move, some person was controlling me.

When he moved me further up I saw ghosts coming to me, they were coming to eat me. I felt a little scared. The person controlling me made me eat power-ups, like apples. Suddenly a ghost was chasing me. The person controlling me managed to get me away, then I got to the end of the maze.

Maximillian Jorge Lunn (9)
St Oswald's Academy, Finningley

The Pen's Adventure

Dear Diary,
Hi my name is Mr Pencil Lead. I started in a warehouse getting painted green but my lead is grey. I'm in a van getting taken to the school. I love it here.

Any lead got broken? No. Then I was going into the scariest place ever, a sharpener! I was going to be even smaller. So I went into a sharpener. It was painful. I had excruciating pain. Then I got snapped. Later on I got put in the bin. Then forgotten about. I was so sad.

Kyle James Williams (9)
St Oswald's Academy, Finningley

Football On The Run

Dear Diary,

I was waiting in the locker room and suddenly I got picked up, I was terrified. The next thing I saw was a huge stadium. A few hours later, people were coming to sit down, I went to sleep for a bit.

The next thing that happened, I was being kicked around. I didn't know what to do...

It was half-time, finally a break. It was the next part of the match, but at least I'd had a break.

Jake Raggett (8)
St Oswald's Academy, Finningley

The Turquoise Pencil

Dear Diary,

This morning, the children galloped in smiling. Oh no! A boy sat down in front of me. Suddenly he grabbed me. Up! Up! Up! My rubber quaked in fear as my petrified face screamed. He rubbed something out on his page. "That tickles," I giggled. My rubber was rubbed on the smooth white page.

A pretty, unusual girl with a gnashing sharpener sat down directly behind me. She sharpened my gorgeous face. Oh the pain. It was terrible. I yelped out in pain. But I guess I should never have trusted her. That is a lesson everyone needs to learn, never trust a pretty girl with a sharpener.

I had a quick chat with my friends, their names are Coloured Pencil, Pen and The Highlighter Gang. A few moments later, two twins, one girl and the other one was a boy, sat down.

Some pencils say if a twin is a girl and the other a boy, they can't be identical. This isn't true because their freckles were in the same place. The two differences I could point out were they had different clothes and the girl had very long hair and the boy had short hair. They both dived for me, picking me up. In a rage, they fought over me.

My rubber and nib officially stretched, On the last pull they snapped me in two. Ouch! Lead dropped out of me and plummeted down, down, down. One of my parts in each of their sweaty hands, they tossed me in the bin laughing hysterically. This is definitely the worst day ever. I was humiliated in front of everyone, sharpened and broken. Hopefully people will learn to look after pencils.
Signed
Turquoise Pencil.

Megan Wright (10)
Totley All Saints CE Primary School, Sheffield

The Roller-Coaster Life Of A School Desk

Dear Diary,

I've had a torturous day (as usual). In the morning it was maths. Johnny was picking his nose, again! But that's not the main problem. It's the fact that he gets his sticky fingers and shoves the putrid-green bogey under me. Luckily, after lunch, Mrs Smith caught him sticking snot on me. As Mrs Smith was telling Johnny off, I was thinking in relief, *no more snot, no more snot*. Plus I might get moved near my best mate Max.

School came to an end (just the end of the day) and as usual the cleaners came in (my favourites). I was eavesdropping on their conversation. Mrs Smith had wanted the cleaner Barbara to try and scrub off the new solid bogeys. She got her cloth and started scrubbing me.

An hour came past, I started to worry. Barbara got up and sighed in dismay and explained that the snot was indestructible and that she couldn't get it off. I was gobsmacked! Mrs Smith just simply said, "Okay, we have got another table at the back and I'll throw this one in the skip."

After ten hours of raging, I still couldn't believe she was going to replace me with that plastic kiddy table.

That evening, I was picked up and put in a small car. It was a very bumpy ride. We reached my future, the skip. I'm a very expensive material but no one seems to care. Before I got chucked in the skip, I said my last words: "I will get revenge one day, Johnny."

Darcy Booth (11)
Totley All Saints CE Primary School, Sheffield

A Diary Of A Boy With A Bed

Dear Diary,
Monday
School was as boring as usual. Did maths - boring. Yoga in PE - boring and finally English - super boring.

Tuesday
OMG I heard something talking at 1 o'clock in the morning... It was my bed! Its deep voice scared me to death. He told me not to be scared. But I wasn't convinced. I said, "How long have you been able to talk?" He spent three hours talking about goffy and crazy stuff and we also made the decision that now we're friends. To sum up, went to school - boring, got back from school - amazing more time with my bed.

Wednesday
It was toy day today, double-whammy, talking bed and toy day. Now all I was thinking in my head was, could I take my bed to school? I had to convince Mum. I shouted, "Mum!"
She shouted back, "Yes."
"Could I take bed to school?" After one hour of fighting and arguing Mum said I could take it.

It took half an hour of pulling my bed to school into the classroom. I showed all my friends about it, then let everyone jump on it but a few people broke a few arms and ribs but that's okay. We went to the paper cupboard where we got our homework and scrunched all of it up. No more homework. We also rang the bell of school so we went home earlier.

Sum up, home - boring, school - amazing (apart from the people who had broken their arms and ribs).

Harrison Corrin (10)
Totley All Saints CE Primary School, Sheffield

Teacher's Mug

Dear Diary,

Where do I start? I'm cracked. My life as a service mug is over. After seven years of being sturdy, I am wounded for life. You wouldn't think that teachers really do their job... All I know is that they have slobbery lips, they slurp really loudly and smell awful. Nerdy teachers! However, they teach you a hell of a lot (I've even had to watch the teacher tut whilst marking seven years of test papers).

Back to the crack... Clumsy George had to barge up and push me off the table and onto the children's carpet. Oh George! I am worried - that pesky, new Sheffield Wednesday mug (the one that Snotty Dotty purchased) - has waited for me to fall apart. He has reached his achievement of being the teacher's mug.

What have I done to deserve this rubbish life? I've always been there when the teacher has needed me most. Hopefully, my replacement is so foul and bad that the teacher has no choice but to take me back. I would laugh so much if that happened. I don't know what I've become! Thinking bad about people just because they are better than me.

It's my time to be forgotten and then cleared out. The bin is my only hope. Except, at the end of term, they have a lost property sale. If I get in it, my service life is back on. But how? I shall keep thinking. Goodbye.

Megan Hill (11)
Totley All Saints CE Primary School, Sheffield

The Incredible Diary Of A Ruler

Dear Diary,

Help me, this crazy boy was throwing me all around the park. I was in more trouble, yuck, this giant pug was chewing me and all his slobber was dripping on me. "Oh thank you." The pug dropped me.

"Uh oh here we go again." Argh the boy was throwing me again, I'm not a stick! Now the pug was chewing me again.

Then I saw rubber chillin'. "Yo rubber." Then rubber (my best friend) said yo. The pug had finally dropped me. What was this? I was stuck in... uh oh a teenage girl was coming. I needed to get out. Too late. Then the weird girl said, "What's this stuck to my foot? Oh it's a ruler, my dad will love this for his work." Uh stubborn people.

Uh this dad has a disgusting beard. OMG this stupid man just snapped my bottom half off and I don't know where it has gone. "Bottom oh bottom, where are you, you stubborn thing? Ahh there you are, got ya. Haha let's glue it on. Oh where will I get the glue from?" Then... rubber came.

I got some glue but the weird glue said, "Put me down."
Ah perfect, now I've got to run and hide before someone else finds me!

Evie Staniforth (10)
Totley All Saints CE Primary School, Sheffield

The Incredible Diary Of A Unicorn Called Pebbles

Dear Diary,
Today the most incredible thing happened to me, I was just taking a sip of fresh water from the glistening lake, when all of a sudden a small girl came walking up to me, she took a deep breath and screamed at the top of her lungs, it was a little frightening to be honest, until she ran up to me and squeezed me. The girl stroked my head gently and told me to follow her, so I did. Soon we arrived at a beautiful cottage next to the calm sea, she skipped inside, so I followed after her. It was very pretty inside the cottage and a sweet scent of blueberry muffins came from the kitchen.
The girl led me into the living room and sat on an armchair was an elderly man. His eyes widened as soon as I stepped in the room, I smiled and wandered over to the armchair, and the man reached out his arm to stroke my fluffy mane. The man climbed on top of me and told me to take him to the magical forest, then he tumbled off my back and limped over to the vast lake. He pointed slowly to a large tree.

Unexpectedly, there stood another unicorn, munching on some emerald green grass. Never ever did I think that I'd meet another unicorn in my life, I thought we were extinct!

Isabel Campsill (11)
Totley All Saints CE Primary School, Sheffield

The Incredible Diary Of... A Piece Of Chewing Gum

Dear Diary,

Today was the most awful day any piece of chewing gum would have ever had to go through. There I was, lying in an imprisoned case (a plastic wrapper), ready to be freed by any innocent stranger to pick me and my buddies up off the shelf.

Seconds later, an overpowering array of sunlight burst into my microscopic, beady eyes. In the blink of an eye, I was snatched from the home that I had lived in for weeks, and then I realised that I would never touch the hands of them again.

Once I was out in the outside world, which didn't last very long, I was immediately plunged into their mouth, and that was when I felt as though I'd never see the light of day again. However, when I entered this deceiving place, it didn't take me long to realise how much they needed me, so I could attempt to make a putrid, rotten mouth in the slightest bit decent again. Using all of my strength, I tried to work my magic on this excruciating disaster.

After being punctured, bruised and torn, I realised my work here was done. I knew that this adventurous event was not going to be my last.

Lily Grayson (11)
Totley All Saints CE Primary School, Sheffield

My Days Of War

Dear Diary,
Today was one like no other. Fighting for all those years and to finally be destroyed. When the war started, it was a time of excitement and expectation, but now I just feel demoralised and just want to go home.
I was only young when I was recruited to the German Army but it is now several years later and it feels like yesterday when I held my first gun. During the battle of Dunkirk, I felt relieved and thought we would win, until I saw all those ships big and small collect the enemy army and sail away to safety. It was as if luck was on their side. I also remember the Battle of Britain when it looked likely that we would conquer the British Isles, when suddenly we received a call to stay put in France and to fight another day. Eventually, when the allies had surrounded our leader (Adolf Hitler) in Berlin, we were told that he had disappeared and at that precise moment I knew they had won. It was all over. We had lost the war and I realised I had been a terrible man. I hope one day I will be able to repay.

Guy Eckersley (10)
Totley All Saints CE Primary School, Sheffield

The Incredible Diary Of A Box!

Dear Diary,
Today I went to the people at 54 Mistletoe Lane. I was delivering some hairspray and a brush. When I got there a small I saw what I thought was a girl called Ariana.

I was opened on a large table. Thankfully Mrs Persons opened me very gently. I was put in a room of glitter, sparkles and pink. Suddenly I was drawn all over with a blue marker. I had wheels and buttons, it was very odd!

The next thing I was pooped on by a smelly baby. I was smelly for the rest of the day.

Then finally, there was peace and quiet for about five seconds. Out of nowhere, some kids came charging through the door. After ten minutes there was quiet again.

Finally, I had no smelly babies, no charging kids, just peace and quiet. Smelly baby thing was going to bed. Ariana and her parents were watching a film. I was finally settling down... Suddenly the smelly baby pooed!

Five minutes later I got back to sleep.

Evie Dastoor (10)
Totley All Saints CE Primary School, Sheffield

A Mobile Phone

Dear Diary,
Today was awful!
This morning Katlin (my owner) headed off to school but left me here all by myself with her putrid little brother (Henry) coming into her room every second of my battery life playing games. Every time he brought me near tiles, I shivered and quaked, praying that he wouldn't drop me. Henry - who was a cold-blooded phone killer, didn't understand that phones could smash, so I was slipping slowly down until... Mum saved the day and caught me.
Sadly, things didn't stay good for long! Henry stomped up the stairs with me in his pocket until I slipped, fell down the stairs and *crash!* I landed screen first onto a tile. Luckily I survived otherwise I would not be telling you this, even though there is a giant crack on my screen. As soon as Katlin got home, she was sobbing her eyes out. Frankly, I should've done the same.

Rachel Holme (11)
Totley All Saints CE Primary School, Sheffield

The Diary Of A Gaming Computer

Dear Diary,

Today me and my owner are moving house and are really excited. At 8 o'clock, my owner picked me up and took me to his car boot, but suddenly he dropped me and I could feel my motherboard in agony as it was cracked and needed replacing. My owner rushed me into the house again and tried turning me on. Nothing happened. Once again, my owner took me outside but instead of taking me to the boot, he took me to the doctor (or the computer specialist as my owner calls it). The doctor told me and my owner that I needed a motherboard transplant and must go into surgery. Now my operation shall start tonight. I need some precious daylight sleep. See you tomorrow!

Sizhe Luo (11)
Totley All Saints CE Primary School, Sheffield

A Car's Day Out

Dear Diary,

Today I have had one of the worst times in my life, I went through a car wash, a hand car wash. It took forever. Until the last parts, which I'll come to later. The car wash took ages. It was like waiting in a queue, to wait in another queue. They scrubbed me with a rock, and then polished me with grease. After this, my owner (Crispiano Chipaldo) complained, so the men explained, "Do you want our special full valet?" My owner said yes, but then realised he shouldn't have because they threw me off a cliff, sliced me in half with a chainsaw and burnt me with a flamethrower.

Samuel Giles (11)
Totley All Saints CE Primary School, Sheffield

Slogman

Dear Diary

This morning I woke up. I rubbed my eyes. But I couldn't see my fingers. I walked to the mine but I didn't know if I was there or not. I think I remember I went to the hospital for a blood transfusion. Unfortunately, they gave me invisibility blood which was going to be fun! I found a Roblox. I got them. They had money in their pocket.

After that I scared my friends, they didn't know I was invisible. I bumped into my friend, Jelly. "Come to my house and play GTA5." We played hide-and-seek and we played Roblox. I needed a drink but I couldn't pick it up. I had my dinner. I had noodles. It was very hard when I went to pick up the spoon. Then I wasn't invisible, I saw my hands and went to the doctors. I opened my hand. I wasn't invisible anymore. I said, "You gave me invisible blood!"

"I am so sorry."

"You should be."

"Was it fun though?"

"Yes, I have to be honest."

I went home and I played a game of GTA5 on my PS. See you later.

Coby Hopkinson (8)
West Meadows Primary School, Hoyland

The Diamond Dolphins

Dear Diary,

Hi, I'm Olivia, what a day I've had! I was playing with my ball and all of a sudden, a weird creature appeared. It seemed like a shark or a dolphin like me. "I hope it is not a clown of me," whispered Nala.

A few minutes later I crept up on the dolphin. Yes, I found out it was a dolphin. She was very kind and helpful but I had to scare her... "Boo! I am so sorry but I had to scare you because you took my ball," angrily said Nala, "but I can find another one for you."

After a while, we finally found a magical diamond ball. "It might bring you good luck," whispered Nala.

"Wow, that sounds amazing!" I said.

"Right, I want it, you can have my colourful ball," said Nala.

"No, I found it first so I get it!" I whispered.

"Let's play with them," said Nala.

"Okay," I shouted.

"Let's go," said Nala.

So I played with the random dolphin, she was always kind and helpful to me and we will always be best friends.

"I will go and find some more friends to come and play with us and you can play with our balls but don't let anyone have them."

"Okay," said Nala.

"See you in a moment," I said but when I went I heard another shark come and get the diamond ball. It was an amazing fright but I saw Nala in a fight. I had to go and help her. I did and she swam away with the blue diamond ball then the shark passed it on to his friend and his friend passed it on to me and he became our friend so he did help us find the diamond and we all played 'come and catch the ball'.

After we played that he said, "Let's play fetch," and then we all had lots of fun so that is the end of my diary entry.

Alisha Moxon (8)
West Meadows Primary School, Hoyland

The Dolphin And The Rainbow Powers

Dear Diary,
One Sunday I was scared because of the storm, it was scaring me really badly. I had to hide away from the storm and someone saw me. I was happy because I was going to swim to a cave that had rainbow water and you get powers when you go inside. I wondered what powers I would get? A few minutes later, it got really dark so I had to go out but suddenly I found out that I had powers and I could make it light enough to see.
Later that day, I was swimming and I found a gold chest but I couldn't open it so I decided to do my magic. What was going on? The chest had lots of buttons in it so I went to the cave again and found a letter that said: 'Come inside'. But I didn't want to but I went in anyway.
A few hours later my flippers had fire in them so I didn't need a torch at all. I just needed to find a key to get through the door but not just any kind of key, a magic key. Would it work?
A year later, I was going to a mine to find the key but I couldn't find it so I used my powers, my fire powers, to see through walls and my rainbow powers so I could pick it up. But I needed water.

Actually, I could get my powers to fetch me down and back up from there and I was thinking I might be able to grab the key and come back up in an elevator so I wouldn't waste my flippers. I thought I might just be able to reach the numbers on the elevator.

When I got back up at the top I put the key in the door and went inside and got some coins then I swam back into the sea and found a gold chest with lots of money and coins. I can make more money with my powers and I can really get more things than I thought I could, I can even get toys. Anyway, I hope that tomorrow it's a lovely day.

Cady Morrison (7)
West Meadows Primary School, Hoyland

The Incredible Diary Of...

Dear Diary,
What a day! All this hassle, I'd been trying to burn down Steve's mansion for over two hours now, this thing was made out of obsidian surely. I had blown up over twelve times so you know what happens when I blow up over twelve times. I become a charged creeper with a lot of superpowers. I get to shoot lava from my mouth and I can spawn loads of other creepers that are dark green and what they do is poison people but they are no use whatsoever.

After an hour I blow up the entire mansion. But Steve was still alive surprisingly but I had this special superpower where I could turn invisible. I didn't want to harm him though so I just went back to my dark, dark cave with a lot of spiders in so I presumed that you wouldn't want to come in.

At six o'clock, it was time for dinner. I had burnt lungs and they were delicious.

After dinner I asked my dad to see if I could go to Jeff's house for a sleepover or two. Dad said I could, "But only for a day." So I got my bag and set off to Jeff's.

Fifteen minutes later, I finally got to Jeff's house. I normally called him J so I'm gonna call him that. J wasn't any regular creeper because he was half creeper and half pig. I know it sounds weird and he sounds you know, dodgy, but he is cool alright, and guess how much money he has? Nine hundred billion pounds! He even has twenty girlfriends! I wish I was him.

We played pool a lot. At night we snuck out and scared some people then we went back to his and went to sleep.

Oliver Jack Turner (8)
West Meadows Primary School, Hoyland

Ariana's Performance Night

Dear Diary,
Last night was the best night ever! Guess what? So I got out of bed and got packing. You ask why? Well, you'll see. What happened was I was going to my concert and a man came up to me.
"I'm Ariana Grande."
"Oh, that famous singer."
"Yes."
"You're my favourite singer."
"Well, it was nice meeting you."
"It was nice meeting you too, bye."
A few minutes later, I had a really long time on the train. I didn't know where to go. I was asking myself questions, where do I go? When will I get there? How many more minutes? What will I do? Where will I go? I have loads more questions. Finally, I got there. I didn't know where to go. I've never been here before. How will I know where to go? I asked a man if he knew where the concert room was. He said he didn't know then I asked another man and he said he didn't know either. Then I asked a woman, she said, "It's just down the road."

I said, "Thank you."

When I got there I went backstage and there were back-up dancers, make-up artists, the boss and there were also decorations. I was so excited I couldn't believe it even though I had done performances before in different countries. Then I sat down in a chair and the make-up artist started doing my hair and make-up then I heard them calling my name. I went home and went to sleep. I woke up at 7am and thought that was a late night!

Charlotte Grace Jones (8)
West Meadows Primary School, Hoyland

Fortnite

An extract

Dear Diary,

On Sunday morning, when I woke up, I was in Fortnite Battle Royale and I waited in the working room. Then... somebody turned the PS4 on and put Fortnite on. A few minutes later, Fortnite loaded and I looked in my locker and it was a mess!

As I looked in my locker, I tried to tidy up but it said I had to get a Victory Royale to tidy up. Could I get a Victory Royale? I fact, I'm just going to start a game.

When I started a game I waited in the Spawn Island and I danced for 10 seconds until we got in the battle bus. As I got in the battle bus I thanked the driver. There were lots of people, there were 100! When I jumped out, I was looking for a place to go and I found a place called Tilted Towers and I dropped to it. As I was dropping down a person shot me. The person who shot me took 50 HP off me.

When I landed I met somebody who was nice and not very good at Fortnite so I made friends with him and we had a battle.

When we got out of Tilted Towers we rifted because of the storm. It was close to us. When we rifted I said, "Come on, come with me."
He said, "Okay."
So we went to Dusty Divot and we had a battle again and then the storm was closing in, we were in peril...

Leon Himsworth (7)
West Meadows Primary School, Hoyland

Olympic Champion 2019

Dear Diary,
I am Ariana Berlin and I love gymnastics, let me tell you about my day.
Earlier, I went to gymnastics to get ready for my competition. It started at 3 o'clock, that was in five minutes...
It was time for the competition.
I spun around and around on the key bars and flipped off the beam. "Wow!" they were cheering for me. It was not scary for me because I have been doing it for ages. Do you think I will get first place? They were calling my name, I best go. "I have done it, I think I nailed it!" I will get the score on Friday.
Later that day, we went to the shop in the car to get some shopping until... we had a car crash! I had to go the hospital and have a metal thing in my leg.
A few hours later, I went in the Olympics! I did a full out, that is two back handsprings with a full twist! I couldn't stick the landing though because of my metal thing in my leg but guess what, I didn't do good, I did great! "I got first place!"

Later that day, when I got home, I couldn't stop thinking about the Olympics and what it would be like to be the world's best gymnastics champion. I loved today, it was the best day ever!

Lily Morgan (7)
West Meadows Primary School, Hoyland

The Incredible Diary Of...
(An extract)

Dear Diary

What a day! I woke up super early, climbed down from my bunk bed to find a strange box at my feet. *What's this?* I wondered. I opened it. Suddenly a huge ball of light spun around me. The light faded and a tiny rat appeared, opened its eyes and blinked, then let out a cute yawn. "It's a rat, it's a mouse, it's a bug mouse!" I screamed. I started throwing books, walkie talkies, more books and pens. It finally stopped still. I caught it in a glass cup. It said, "Oh if that makes you feel safer my name is Rati and I'm your Kwami. I can transform you into a superhero."
"But why?" I asked. "Okay, let me just ask my mum if I can do that first..."
"No, no, no!" shouted Rati. "I have got to be a secret."
"Look there is a super villain coming to Paris."
"All you have to say to transform is Rati, pink on!"
"Rati, pink on!" I shouted. Rati jumped into the earrings.
When I opened my eyes I was in a hero costume with weapons and everything.

"Rati, wherever you are I want my normal clothes back!"

Georgia Holly Marsh (8)
West Meadows Primary School, Hoyland

Lionel Messi And Ronaldo Of The World

Dear Diary,

Best day ever! I was in the playground and I was talking with my friend. "Do you believe that the footballer, Messi, is real bro?" I said.

"Yes, obviously he is, who got the sick goal on Saturday!" shouted my friend.

"What? Why, don't you think Ronaldo is not good?" I replied.

"Okay then, meet me at 3 o'clock at the park."

"Okay," I said.

Later that day... "Okay, I don't see him!" I shouted.

"I'm right here, clean your eyes, dude!" said my friend. "Let's have a football match!"

"Okay then I'm Ronald here!" I said.

"Okay, I'm Messi, I bet Messi is better than Ronaldo!" said my friend.

"But I bet Ronaldo is better than Messi, I bet!"

So we had a football match, we turned into Ronaldo and Messi. At half-time in the match Ronaldo quickly got a goal and after the half-time Messi got a goal. We were tied.

Later, when the match finished we said well done to each other and lived happily ever after.

Keira Grace Pepper (8)
West Meadows Primary School, Hoyland

The Incredible Diary Of...

Dear Diary,
That was the worst day ever. Do you want to hear what happened? You do? Well then, it was a normal day, a Saturday, when I heard my son Max crying. I quickly ran downstairs and went into the garden. I found Max lying on the grass. Ben stood laughing. "Lily, what's your point of the story?" I asked Lily who was playing with them.
"Well, we were playing. I was the princess, Max was the knight and Ben was the dragon." She gave me a look to tell me what happened. I took Max inside and told him to play with Evie.
A few minutes later, I went upstairs to see what they were playing. I found Max standing in a pretty pink princess dress. I took the dress off him. Jasper came home to look after Max.
After that I went shopping for bread, milk and some sweet treats. So I went to the shop but when I came out of the shop it started raining. I had to run but which way? I'd forgotten, oh no, but then something hit me... A paper aeroplane. It was a map and I soon found my way home.

Myla Fannan (7)
West Meadows Primary School, Hoyland

Pokémon: The Journey Begins

Dear Diary,

Yesterday I got into my bed on the streets. I wondered if anyone would find me or if I would be a wild Pikachu as I dozed off to sleep.

When I woke up this morning a trainer was carrying me. Then she said, "I'm your new trainer, let's get lots of Pokémon shall we?" I was so happy. She said, "Let's get that Eevee." She threw a Pokéball at it and she caught it.

Then we went to a gym. I went first. The gym leader got Charmander out of her Pokéball and he used flamethrower and I used thunderbolt. I jumped up and I jumped down and used it and won.

When we came out we saw a Snivy, an Oshawott and a Caterpie and caught all three of them. Then Team Rocket came. The trainer used Oshawott and Caterpie. Caterpie used so much energy it evolved into Butterfree and beat Team Rocket and went to a group of Butterfree.

We were so happy!

Calum Warren (8)
West Meadows Primary School, Hoyland

The Incredible Diary Of...

Dear Diary,

Today I went to McDonald's with my friends. We had some fun and we talked about it all the way home. When we got home we played GTA5. We were police on GTA5. I said to my friends, "Do you want to go to the cinema?"

My friends said, "Okay, shall we watch Star Wars?"

I said, "Okay," so we went to watch Star Wars. After we'd watched Star Wars we had KFC for dinner, it was so much fun. My friends went back home so I played some more GTA5. We then watched another film.

We went to a cafe and I had pancakes for tea. I said to my mum, "Did you like it?"

My mum said it was good.

I said to my dad, "Did you like it?"

"It was really good," he said.

Fynley Blade Young (8)
West Meadows Primary School, Hoyland

Party Night

Dear Diary,

I woke up and I realised that I was not in the water anymore and I saw my friend in the water but then something happened to me. I waved my tail and put myself back in the water.

I was feeling happy because I had the pool to myself which makes me happy because the pool is very wavy.

The next day the water was changing different colours. It changed to red, light green, pink to light blue, dark blue to yellow, dark red to dark green and light purple to dark purple.

"A ball," I said, "we'll play with it now so we can have a party."

I need some sleep after that party but that party was fun. I'm going to do it again.

Claudia McDonald (8)
West Meadows Primary School, Hoyland

The Incredible Diary Of...

Dear Diary,
What a day! I got up then I went outside to eat my breakfast. I went for a walk, like half a mile!
An hour later, I found a door. I went around the door but nothing was there so I went back because it was getting super dark. I made it morning with my magic. I went back to the door again and it was open so I went in and it was full of mushrooms. "This is amazing," said Pegasus.
At midnight, I found Rat Girl and the bad guy. The bad guy was trying to steal Rat Girl's earrings. I transformed into Fox Girl and I helped Rat Girl fight the bad guy.
At bedtime, I ran home as fast as I could.

Paige Manners (8)
West Meadows Primary School, Hoyland

The Incredible Diary Of...

Dear Diary,

I am a megalodon, I live in the Pacific Ocean. I'm the biggest creature in the ocean. One day a submarine came close to me so I bit it with my humongous teeth. I went to find food and found a whale. I crunched it up and ate it up in one go. I am terrifying.

After, I swam into a big net. I was caught up but I wanted to get free so I bit through the net. I am free!

Alfie Briggs (7)
West Meadows Primary School, Hoyland

Charlie's Adventures: The Missing Money Thief!

Dear Diary,

I had an atrocious day, let me tell you why.

Me and my dad went to the bus station. In a split second a weird person came and took a handful of money out of my dad's pocket without him knowing. I asked my dad, "Do you have any money left?" While my dad put his fingers in his pocket he realised that there wasn't any money left. We told an officer that someone had stolen our money. The officer said, "Oh dear."

I told my dad once again and I asked, "Dad, where should we sleep?"

My dad replied, "I don't know."

As we walked outside I noticed a £100. We spent it trying to get home. While we were waiting a man came and asked, "Will you give me some money?" My dad said, "No!"

Then a man came and told us to fight. While we ran around this awful, smelly bus like animals the bus driver stopped the bus and kicked us out. I asked, "Dad, what should we do?"

We were halfway through the journey when I sat down. My dad decided that we should run. I said, "Run, it's about a mile!"
We ran home. What an adventure!
Charlie.

Daniel Saukaitis (11)
Worsbrough Bank End Primary School, Worsbrough Dale

The Rose Bush Adventure

Dear Diary,
Today was quite interesting but let's begin at the beginning...
It was a normal Saturday morning until a van pulled up outside the castle. I thought it might just be a visitor.
Then, all of a sudden, the man with the van started cutting out my roots, luckily he didn't hurt me. But I thought he was bushnapping me! When he was lowering me in his van and he was shutting the doors I prayed for this to be a dream.
Then everything was pitch-black, every second in the ancient van felt like months but as my life flashed before my eyes I heard a click, it was the door. The door shut.
It turned out that it wasn't someone saving me, the door wasn't shut properly. All of a sudden I started sliding to the doors, we were on a hill! I was terrified then I was falling. Then I crashed.
I thought nothing could get any worse, I was screaming and I guess someone heard because I was bushnapped again but this time they put me in a sack.

I fell asleep and when I woke up I had been hooked up to a machine but when I read their name tag it said 'CIA'.
I hope I can go home soon,
The Rose Bush.

Lilyblue Monteith Walker (11)
Worsbrough Bank End Primary School, Worsbrough Dale

The Pirate Attack

Dear Diary,
I had a disgusting day with my flying...
It started with my Sunday morning as usual, flying through the sky across the nature-filled island. Soon I met a lonely cloud. I thought to help until... an explosion went above my head. The sky made a shattering movement. I went white.
After a while, the sound of a gravelly voice said, "Oh, Peter, where are you?" I straight away knew it was the pirates that had come for revenge but I wondered why. Then I knew why... I had destroyed their ship. I will never forget that! I quickly dashed to the dreadful pirate crew. I shouted at them, "You will never catch me alive!" The cannon moved wherever I went! I had a plan to distract them though. I told them to face where they were going. Suddenly, guess what happened? Did they crash or did they not crash? If you said crash, you're right! The ship collapsed slowly.
I flew to the lonely cloud again. What will happen tomorrow? I don't know! Will they come back or not?

What an adventurous day I had defeating them. Let's have fun next time.
Peter Pan.

David Saukaitis (11)
Worsbrough Bank End Primary School, Worsbrough Dale

The Incredible Diary Of... Where's Wally?

Dear Diary,
Today has been one of the weirdest days I've ever had.
I was just doing my daily routine, picking my clothes and brushing my teeth until people started knocking at the door. It was only 6am so I didn't have a clue what they were doing about at this time, people try to find me all the time, it's very weird.
It happened in lots of places like in a different country, it feels like playing hide-and-seek or something, I've been to lots of places like Egypt and Spain and so on.
I feel curious because I always have to hide behind objects. I don't really think about what to do anymore because everyone keeps following me, watching. I don't know whether I should be afraid of something.
So one hour later I entered a forest where I could hide better and keep safe because those people looked like creeps.

I didn't know this but I entered a dangerous forest because there were deadly creatures inside so, up ahead I saw a tiger. I ran back home and got safe. Wally.

Connor Paul Williams (11)
Worsbrough Bank End Primary School, Worsbrough Dale

Harry Potter: Detention Death

28th July, 2008
Dear Diary,
I (Harry Potter) woke up with Ron and Hagrid looking over me. Scared me to death! I asked them why I was there but all they said was that I passed out in detention, and because I was in detention that I would be going into the Enchanted Forest. Thirty minutes later, just after we had got into the forest, lots of Dementors started shooting their bows and arrows at us. Because we were running, we didn't realise where we were.
Anyway, let me get to the point... Hagrid's brother - a giant called Burt - jumped out to save us and got hit 114 times on the body. That's when I started to get mad and I made some of the Dementors' bows fly. I made some of the Dementors disappear, so they all got scared and ran away. Also, the dog got shot but he survived. Ron was absolutely scared to death. We unfastened Burt and took him back to Hagrid's so I used one of my spells to dig a hole.
See ya!
Harry Potter.

Thomas Adam Elbourne (10)
Worsbrough Bank End Primary School, Worsbrough Dale

Sergeant William: Out At War

Dear Diary,

Today has been such a shock. I'm not really good at spelling but you should understand me. Well, let's get into it.

I had a fight on the battlefield, this only happened because in 1928 I joined the British forces.

Me and Mark got out of the trenches this morning and had the battle of our lives. The day got harder and harder and at 7:15pm I got shot in the leg and Laurant, our first aider, came and treated me. As I'd got shot in the leg I wasn't allowed to battle for an hour and after that hour had gone I was straight back on the dreadful battlefield.

It was coming to midnight, I was getting tired, I got called back to the trenches to get some sleep. Before I went to sleep I had something to eat because I hadn't eaten all day. At around 3:34am my officer woke me up because a present arrived from my mum and dad. In the present there were some new pens so I could write this.

See you soon, Sergeant William.

Joel Bobby Besau (10)
Worsbrough Bank End Primary School, Worsbrough Dale

Grubby Gertrude's First Day At School

Dear Diary,
Today was my first day at my new school. Urgh! Even thinking about it makes me bored.
I woke up, well only because the piles of rubbish were sticking into my back. Well anyway, I threw on my new dungarees (well they didn't look new). After, I swam through rubbish to get to my door. I didn't brush my teeth but I did put some effort in. I tried to brush my hair but the brush got stuck. Oh well! I found a piece of melted chocolate in my pocket which I ate for breakfast. I walked to school but flies were trying to eat my chocolate.
I didn't make any friends and the teacher told me to leave the class. I was sent to the head teacher because of the stench coming off of me. Rude! Why does this always happen to me?
I got sent home. I'm not allowed back till I'm clean. Urgh! Not another school.
Gertrude.

Demi-May Williams (11)
Worsbrough Bank End Primary School, Worsbrough Dale

The Incredible Diary Of... The Delivery Driver

Dear Diary,

Today has not been a good one. I was late for my delivery - that's the first time I've been late. Delivering to the hungry hogs in World War 2. And even worse, my order was from... no-man's-land. I did not know if they would kill me (I was scared). I was speeding through traffic until I got there. I was told she was dead. I had to take her place in the war!

I put on her blood-soaked gear and it was an AK-47 with a dress and armour. I thought I was going to die but luckily I was wrong... See you tomorrow.

The delivery driver in a dress.

Hamish Monteith Walker (11)
Worsbrough Bank End Primary School, Worsbrough Dale

Young Writers Information

We hope you have enjoyed reading this book – and that you will continue to in the coming years.

If you're a young writer who enjoys reading and creative writing, or the parent of an enthusiastic poet or story writer, do visit our website **www.youngwriters.co.uk**. Here you will find free competitions, workshops and games, as well as recommended reads, a poetry glossary and our blog. There's lots to keep budding writers motivated to write!

If you would like to order further copies of this book, or any of our other titles, then please give us a call or order via your online account.

Young Writers
Remus House
Coltsfoot Drive
Peterborough
PE2 9BF
(01733) 890066
info@youngwriters.co.uk

Join in the conversation!
Tips, news, giveaways and much more!

YoungWritersUK   @YoungWritersCW